KISSING Navy

KISSING NAVY

Plump Playwright Act V

Alone and lonely, baker and romance author Navy turns to her childhood friend for sexual research, not expecting him to crash on her doorstep, help her woo a local fireman, purchase a hunting lodge, and steal her heart from under her.

Oliver's home to win the heart of his childhood friend Navy now that she's grown up and all woman. How will he convince her to give up on the fireman and date him instead?

KISSING NAVY

Plump Playwright Act V

by Sevannah Storm

This is a work of fiction. The characters, incidents and dialogues in this book are of the author's imagination and are not to be construed as real. Any resemblance to actual events or persons, living or dead, is completely coincidental.

Published by Sevannah Storm.

~~~

First Edition 2022

Cover Art by Sevannah Storm and Kiki Smith

https://www.sevannahstorm.com/

Version_1
~~~

Also by Sevannah Storm

The Blood of Legends Series

The Huntress

The Healer

*

The Gifting Series

Soul Forged

Fate Forged

Sun Forged

War Forged

Star Forged

Shadow Forged

Earth Forged

Lust Forged

Fire Forged

*

The Qaldreth Warriors

Sol Survivor

Dark Survivor (Coming soon)

*

The Space Hunter Chronicles

The Shikari

The Justisaar

*

Inkounter Series
Inkoded

*

Standalones
Xiaxan Fox

Ire of Silver

The Crucible of the Eternal

*

Plump Playwright Series
Plump Jane

Seducing Amelia

Loving Finley

Keeping Tessa

Kissing Navy

Prologue

WHAT DOES IT FEEL like when a woman runs her tongue from your balls to the tip of your cock?

Oliver blinked at the text. What the hell? He checked the number and hardened, as he always did with thoughts of Navy. Pining for his childhood friend was pathetic, yet no matter what he did, he couldn't stop himself.

His fingers trembled as he typed. *Why do you want to know? And hello, by the way.*

Oli, please, help me. I'm writing a novel, so you can't say anything to Gray. He'll just tease me until I want to kill him. Brothers. Love them. Hate them. Hello to you too.

Having just dried himself from a shower and yanked a pair of sweatpants on, Oliver sprawled on his bed, rested a hand on his chest, and dialed her.

"I'm sorry. You're the only man I can ask." Her husky voice rolled over his senses.

He gritted his teeth against her sensual allure. After eight years, he'd yet to find her equal. Instead, he settled for scraps, wishing every woman he dated was her.

"As long as I get a copy?" he teased, struggling to maintain the illusion, that of her brother's best friend.

"But what if I suck at writing?"

"Let me be the judge. Mm, now to your question. How to put this..." Rubbing his chest, he raised his gaze to the ceiling where shadows played across its white surface. "Her tongue is hot and wet, and if she swirls it around my balls, intense tingles ripple outward, rushing, along with her lick, to the tip of my cock." He cleared his throat. Hell, never had he imagined being in this position. Lowering his hand, he cupped his hard-on through his pants. An answering wave of tingles mimicked his words. "When she sucks, the pleasure is intense, and I struggle to breathe."

"Any tightness in the chest?"

Heat uncoiled in his belly. "Yes, and something in my gut, like I'm doing crunches."

She hummed, and the clatter of keys from a keyboard almost drowned her voice. "What thoughts are running through your head?"

Thoughts? No, images, and they flooded him now. Navy and her curly black hair, her bright blue eyes, and her smile that shone like a thousand suns. He'd last seen her four years ago at his mother's funeral, delicious curves barely hidden behind slacks and a button-up blouse. She'd filled out, her sixteen-year-old figure had hinted at the woman she would become.

The tap-tap of typing preceded her next words. "Or are they images? I read that men are more visual."

He groaned. Navy sprawled beneath him, her hooded eyes, her parted mouth as she chanted his name in her husky voice. He visualized the shape of her breasts, the shade of her nipples, and shuddered.

"Yes." His voice was hoarse like gravel meeting tarmac. *Shit. She can't ever know how I yearn for her.*

"I like that." She sighed. "Thanks, Oli. Would you mind if I bother you in the future...for research?"

He slipped his hand inside his pants and rubbed his hard-on, swallowing a groan. Had she been beside him, he would be balls deep in her now. "Never. Bother away."

"You're the best. Kisses." And she hung up, leaving him rock hard and unfulfilled.

Kisses, sucks, hugs, and fucks, that's what he wanted from her. But it had to come with her heart. Tossing his phone aside, he rolled out of bed for another shower. If he was going to jerk off, it might as well be where he could clean up afterward.

~*~

Five months later.

Oliver palmed the book Navy had sent him. A novella with a plump woman on the cover, a brunette, with sensual curves just like Navy's. *Hounding Hannah* was the title. He flipped it over to read the blurb.

Hannah has a comfortable life writing her romance novels and walking her apartment building's dogs. She has one man in her life, and by in her life, she means watching him from her apartment windows.

Mr. Ripped is gorgeous, switching between working in his office and workouts in his lounge. She sees him on her dog walks, but her embarrassment over her plump backside prevents her from approaching him. That is until a dog escapes and forces her to run pell-mell through the park and into Mr. Ripped out for a jog.

Through his telescope, Roman is fascinated by the woman in the apartment across from him. With her curves and her penchant for doing Kegel exercises while eating cookies, he can't dismiss his interest. When she sprawls before him in the park, he finally has the opportunity to meet her.

A friendship like warm socks forms, except it's the curve of her cheek, the plumpness of her bottom lip, the sweetness of her smile that torments him.

Now he needs to convince her she's more than enough woman for him.

Late for a meeting with his personal banker, Oliver dared do nothing more. But instead of leaving, he flipped the pages to read page one of the first chapter. When his phone rang, he was three chapters in and engrossed, loving the quirky woman named Hannah and her crazy life. Navy's personality saturated each page, and he couldn't get enough of it.

"I'm on my way," he answered without checking caller I.D. "Or better yet, can we postpone it to tomorrow?" After his banker's agreement, Oliver hung up, shrugged out of his jacket, and lowered himself onto the couch, taking a second to prop his feet on the coffee table.

~*~

A few months later.

"Oli?"

Oliver's breath caught at Navy's husky voice. Lust slammed into him like a solid wall of heat. He tightened his hold on his phone.

"Navy... Give me a sec." He held the phone to his chest. "Get me the costs for them all."

His assistant, Jay, nodded, folded the papers into its file, and left.

Pushing out of his leather chair, Oliver faced the window and lifted his phone to his ear. "What do you need, Blue?"

"Am I bothering you? I can call back."

An urge to hug her pierced his chest, and he rubbed the ache while forcing a chuckle. "You never bother me."

She hesitated. "Are you sure?"

"Navy," he growled.

"Fine." She huffed. "Okay, this one's a different sort of question. Have you ever been in love?"

He stilled. A thick ball of fiery emotion lodged in his throat, pressing at the backs of his eyes.

"Oli, you there? Holy sugar, I've lost him."

"I'm—" He cleared his throat. "I'm here. And yes."

"How did it feel?"

Did? He winced. Leaving her and his home had done nothing but deepen the pain. "It's agony, and as every year passes, it worsens." He rested his temple on the cool glass and closed his eyes.

She squeaked. "Why? Isn't love supposed to be sweet-smelling roses and bright sunshine?"

He snorted. "She doesn't know, has no idea."

Navy gasped. "If you tell her—"

"Unrequited." He sighed.

Navy grumbled, slamming something down. "Any woman would be lucky to have you, Oli."

Any woman but the one he wanted. "Right."

"I could talk some sense into her." There was a hard edge to her voice, as if she was angry on his behalf. He liked that.

"Oh? And what would you say?" He grinned. What would his oldest friend say about him?

"You want a list?" She hummed. "You're kind, loyal, helpful, um, handsome..."

He chuckled. She thought him handsome. That was a good start. "You're describing a dog, Blue."

She laughed. The unrestrained joy of it engulfed him and summoned his smile. He winked at his reflection in the glass.

"I am. I'm sorry. Did you get my book?"

"I did, and I loved it."

She gulped. "You read it?"

Read it? He had her releases on notification. As soon as she launched a book, he bought it. Three so far, but he'd loved each one. In the darkness of night, when he ached for her, he reread certain scenes, those that revealed her character the most. He tapped his temple on the glass. He was a lovesick fool.

"Anything for my Blue." He gritted his teeth. *Quit gushing.*

"Ditto. Besides, I owe you...*big.*"

"Dinner?" An invisible hand squeezed his heart at the idea of seeing her again.

She squealed. "You're coming home?"

Home? Yes, she was his home. He'd been away far too long. "Thinking about it."

"But why? Your dad moved south, right? Somewhere warm."

"Colefield is in my blood. I miss it." *Miss you.* In all this time, he'd yet to form a game plan with regards to wooing her. Everything else had lined up perfectly, but he still didn't have a strategy to win Blue.

"I'd love to see you." And she meant it. She wouldn't lie. Everything about her was an open book. "Will Gray be coming with you?" The hope in her voice sliced through Oliver.

"Sorry, Blue, he's in Africa somewhere."

"Well, that's fine too, I guess." Sadness saturated her words. "You're staying with me, right?"

Oliver's breath hitched. *Stay with her? In her home? A door away from her bed?* "Sure." He couldn't say no. She'd wonder why and wouldn't understand unless he explained how he felt. Avoiding her so far hadn't worked, but he didn't have the balls to reveal all. Not yet.

"Dinner's on me then." She chuckled. "I'll make your favorite."

He smiled. "And what would that be?"

"Elk Shepherd's Pie."

He blinked back tears. His mother would treat them once a month for Sunday brunch.

"I used to watch your mom make it, remember? I loved being in the kitchen with her. She'd have fifties music playing and her hair in curlers while she danced between stove, fridge, and sink."

"You were the daughter she always wanted, Blue." His mom had made him notice how well Navy had filled out, how pretty her blue eyes and bright smile were. Until then, he'd thought of her as his best friend's little sister, nothing more.

"Thanks, Oli," Navy rasped then sniffed. "So, I'll see you when I see you?" She forced a stiff laugh. "I know better than to ask either of you for a fixed date."

It'll be soon. "True." He'd talk to Gray. Maybe it was time he came home to visit his family.

"I'll text you my address."

He huffed. "I think I can remember where you live, Blue."

"It's been nine years, Oli. I sold my family home."

Pain wrenched his stomach. "Why?"

"Too big for just me. I needed something closer to town and finding myself stranded in mid-winter was never fun."

Ice slid down his neck. He clenched his hand around his phone. That she'd been alone, scared, in danger pierced him. Not once had he thought she wouldn't be well or safe. How he felt solidified his intentions. It was now or never. If he didn't pursue this, he'd never get over her, never move on.

"Holy sugar, cupcakes are done. Got to go, Oli. Chat later." She hung up, leaving him hard, sad, lonely, and determined to see her.

Maybe when he gazed upon her heart-shaped face, he'd realize they wouldn't suit? He could hope. Maybe when she saw him, she would return his love? He snorted. Improbable. He was such an idiot to hope otherwise.

Chapter One

IN ROMANCE, THE FIRST kiss had to hit all the feels: his gentle touch, the intensity in his eyes, his shuddering breath. Missing the mark messed up the novel for Navy which was why she was stumped. Flipping her industrial oven open, she grabbed the tray and yelped.

"Gloves!" Cursing herself for her lack of focus, she held her burned fingers under the cool water, sighing when the sting lessened. As the only baker in small-town Colefield, burning herself was an occupational hazard.

"Navy," she grumbled, remembering the oven mitts on before pulling out the last batch of vanilla, rose-flavored cupcakes.

The Ladies Forum was holding its biweekly meeting. If she didn't hurry, twelve women would starve to death. Which was why she'd been asked to bake three dozen cupcakes. While the last batch cooled, she mixed icing sugar in a variety of flavors: salted caramel, orange chocolate, coconut and pineapple, tasting each one until sweetness clenched her cheeks.

Despite her well-rounded curves, she didn't like sweet things. Sure, chocolate had its place, but a plate of fries, buttered popcorn, or a cheeseburger were far more enticing than cheesecake.

Wiping her hands on her apron, she dripped food coloring into the bowls of readymade icing sugar: pink, orange, yellow, and blue. After mixing them individually, she scooped each one into its own piping bag and decorated the cupcakes with flicks of her wrist.

She stacked them into bakery crates, and with one last glance at the massive clock above the stove, she tore off her apron and hairnet, yanked her jacket on, and scooped up the snow machine's keys. She loaded the crates onto the back of the machine in quick trips to the garage. Then with a scarf strangling her and a beanie squashing her curls, she sped to the town hall.

The quickest route was between houses and not along the gravel-lined roads. Since her bakery was undergoing renovations, her massive ovens were in her home. Commuting was easier along with locking up after a long day. Now she was home and could take a nap while her goodies baked. When the bakery reno was done, she'd have a coffee shop too. She huffed a cloud of frozen breath through her scarf. Orders had upped, counteracting the drop in walk-ins. Folks still needed their morning croissant. She just delivered now.

"Ah, bacon, cheese…" she hummed, steering the machine over the dips and skidding to a halt amid a cloud of white powder. "Coffee."

Someone had salted the steps and a little of the walkway. She stumbled a bit then sprinted inside the hall.

"Ah, there you are, Navy." Ms. Beeman grinned, hurrying ahead of Navy to ensure there was enough space on the overladen table for the 'delectables.'

"Are you staying for tea?" Mrs. Fitzpatrick waddled closer, but when she reached for a caramel cupcake, Ms. Beeman smacked her hand.

Navy smothered a chuckle behind a cough at Mrs. Fitzpatrick's disgruntled expression. "I wish I could, Ms. B. I've got to get started on Mason's spiderman cake." Which was an outright lie. That she'd finished first thing this morning, but spending hours listening to the same gossip wasn't Navy's cup of tea, so to speak.

Mrs. Fitzpatrick, as the school nurse, sucked in a shaky breath and raised a gnarled finger, about to regale Navy on Mason's crazy antics. "Oh, dear, that boy—"

"—is turning ten," Ms. Beeman hurried to say. As the school's principal, she arched a pointed brow at Mrs. Fitzpatrick. "He'll grow up to be such a charmer."

"Loser," Mrs. Fitzpatrick coughed and met Ms. B's glare with an innocent flutter of her eyelashes.

"Since you and the Landons have been friends since kindergarten, will you be attending *that* party?" Ms. Beeman tidied the cups by spinning them so that the handles pointed in the same direction.

"Too busy. I have pies and bread to bake for Milly's, Christmas cakes for the Haven Retirement Village, and a wedding cake." Navy frowned. It *was* too much, but as the only baker, there wasn't anyone else to do it. Milly's standard order subsidized her income, but baking bread wasn't glamorous or as creative as a wedding cake.

"And don't forget the standard order of cupcakes for the fire station." Mrs. Fitzpatrick wiggled her bushy eyebrows.

"Of course." Navy met the old school nurse's knowing look, willing herself not to blush.

"Have you heard about the hunting lodge?" Ms. Beeman gripped a spoon and stabbed the crystallized sugar in its pot. "It was sold along with acres around it. Word has it, the owner means to market it to those city folk eager to shoot something."

"Elk?" Navy squeaked, pinched her lips, and struggled to rein in her anger.

Muttering a hasty goodbye, she barreled out of the hall and leapt onto her snow machine. She didn't like the idea of strangers hunting animals that fed the starving families in Colefield. Extra hunters meant less food for those needing the meat.

She skidded the snow machine on the snow-laden verge outside the fire station. Its massive roller doors gaped, laughter reaching her from the back. She whipped off her beanie and scarf, fluffed her hair, then grabbed the last crate, eager to feast her eyes on Antony Young. Tall with brown hair flopping over his temple and deep brown eyes were enhanced by a muscled torso and an easy smile. He was by the far the handsomest bachelor in Colefield.

Every single woman in town would throw herself at anything with a working cock. Navy grimaced at her thoughts. Men were scarce, and perhaps loneliness drove them as much as it did Navy. But where they used their bodies in the hopes of finding their happily-ever-after, she baked. The way to a man's heart was through his stomach, right? She chuckled. If that was true, there'd be a line of admirers from her front door to the town hall.

"Cupcakes! Get your fix right here," she called as she marched into the station.

Chief Max Henderson came out first, poking his head through his office door. More of the guys streamed out, helping themselves to a cupcake. Antony was last, sauntering over with his hands shoved into the pockets of his fire dex pants.

She sighed at his white sleeveless T-shirt hugging an impressive chest and offered a smile, relying on her professional mask to save her.

"Hi, Navy, how are things?" He stood a little close to her while he chose a cupcake.

"Good, as usual." She cleared her throat, hating the slight warble in her voice. "And you?"

What she should do is ask him out. Problem is, every time she opened her mouth to do so, no words formed. Her tongue tangled something fierce.

"Good." He bit into the caramel cupcake and grinned, icing sugar on his upper lip. With a swipe of his thumb, he caught the dollop and popped it into his mouth. "Until next week?"

She nodded, snapped the empty crate shut, and bolted for the lonely safety of her snow machine. As she careened away, she chastised herself, muttering at her lack of courage. Her assistant, Tina, was kneading bread when she arrived home.

"Hey." Navy slapped her beanie on her jeans. "Thanks for starting."

"Sure, since you pay me to." Tina grinned, her white-blonde hair standing up like she'd stuck her finger in a power socket. "Same as last week? No dinner invitation."

"Don't you know it," Navy huffed, pouring too much soap on her hands at the sink.

"Made you a three-cheese grilled sandwich." Tina pointed at the microwave with her elbow—the only part of her not covered in flour.

"Ah, you're a lifesaver." Navy dried her hands on her jeans and snatched the plate out of the microwave. She bit into the sandwich with a groan.

"And you didn't ask him?" Tina sighed. "No, don't bother answering that. You'd be bouncing out of your skin if he said yes and dragging your lip on the floor if he said no. Since you're doing neither..."

"Yeah, rub it in. I used to be bolder than this," Navy whined around a mouthful of salty, gooey goodness. "Once I'm done eating, I'll deliver Mason's cake." She pointed with the sandwich at the cake box on a side counter.

"Leaving the bread and pies to me?" Tina didn't look up from her kneading.

"For now." Navy shrugged. "I'll bake a few loaves while I ice the wedding cake."

"Don't forget I'm leaving early. It's Lisa's birthday."

"I remember. And your anniversary too?" Biting on her sandwich to hold it in place, Navy grabbed the envelope tucked in the utensil drawer. "Got you this," she mumbled.

Tina hurried to wash her hands but frowned when she took the envelope. She flipped it open and gaped. "You didn't." She danced on the spot as she pulled out two plane tickets to the Bahamas. "It's for next week. Are you sure, Navy? Don't you need me?"

"I can cope without you for a week, Tina." She resisted rolling her eyes. "Lisa covered the resort and organized your passports."

"I was wondering about that." Tina beamed then threw her arms around Navy, squeezing her half to death. "Best surprise ever," she squealed, deafening Navy in the process.

"Good, glad you love it. Now, can I finish my sandwich?"

With her hands once more in bread dough, Tina calmed enough to talk about orders that had come in via email. "One birthday cake for six-year-old Kevin, a rocket or something spacey. And Nanette's bridal shower is this weekend."

Navy winced. "Sugarplums, forgot about that."

She was hoping she'd have time to visit her mom and do some writing. Her editor was expecting the next novel in the series. And she also wanted to rewrite *Hounding Hannah*. She'd come a long way since then and was considering turning it into a series about a plump author (herself), writing about a plump author falling in love who wrote about a plump author...well, falling in love.

It sure as sugar-honey-ice-tea wasn't going to be her if she had to do the asking. Antony had been an inch from her. A whole inch. And he'd done nothing. Made no indication, didn't *accidentally* touch her, just ate her cupcake and left. If that was a euphemism, she wasn't getting it.

She was going to be that lonely, epically horny, old woman, selling her fantasies while having an intense relationship with her seventy-fifth dildo named Reginald. Slumping, she slithered off the stool and placed her plate in the sink.

"I'll do an all-nighter and get them done. Tomorrow morning, you do the deliveries while I crash."

Tina squeaked. "Even the wedding cake?"

"Sure. A day early shouldn't be an issue." Navy filled a glass with water, downed it, then grabbed the snow machine's keys. "You finish the bread, and what you don't get to, just jot on the board. I'm going to check in on my baby after I drop off Mason's cake."

And by baby, she meant her bakery, Sugar Momma's. She was eager to see what progress Eric had made with the bespoke counter.

Chapter Two

Oli? If you're awake, please call.

Oliver stared at Navy's text, then glanced at the clock. Two? What was she doing up that late? He huffed. Not that he should judge, but he had a valid excuse. He couldn't sleep.

He dialed. "Hey, Blue."

"Oli, I'm stumped. Stuck in this silly scene." She sounded stressed, tired, and desperate. If he was there, she'd be up for another reason.

He scowled. "Breathe. What's the matter? And why are you up so late?"

"Too many orders I need to get out. I want to do nothing this weekend except sleep and write." She chuckled. "Probably not going to happen, but I can try, right?" She yawned. "I thought I'd write a little while things are in the oven." She mumbled, "Maybe I should've napped instead. Too late."

"Fuck, what you need is someone to spank your ass."

She squealed. "Oh. Love that. I could work that in."

He groaned and rubbed his cock. Damn fool woman putting ideas in his tortured mind. "Have you ever been spanked? You can't exactly write about it if you've never experienced it."

"Good point. Holy sugar, I'm back to square one." She tapped something hard. "What if I switch to his point of view? Have you spanked someone, Oli?"

The eagerness in her voice sliced through his anger, and he slumped. Why did he do this to himself?

Because he damned well loved her.

"Yes." He squeezed his eyes shut and let his fantasies run wild. "What do you want to know?"

"Do you get aroused by the act?"

He'd taken to stroking his cock. Sighing, he tucked his arm behind his head. It wouldn't bode well for their courtship if she realized he jerked off during their phone calls. She tempted him though, with talks of love, orgasms, and spankings.

"Not from the act of hurting her, no, but from her reactions, the way her body arches, her hisses and moans, how wet she becomes."

"Mm, my man must do that for me, just once."

He sat up. "Your man?"

"Yeah, wherever the ass is. I'm making a list."

Relieved he had no competition, he lay down and smiled. "Let me hear this list."

She chuckled. "Sure. Tallish, but not seven feet. That would be silly paired against my height. Strong body, mind, and self-disciplined is such a turn-on." She mumbled, "His kisses must singe my socks. I want to be all aflutter in his presence. His every gesture must spark something in me."

"Every gesture?" He grinned.

"Yeah, the way he wraps his fingers around a mug. When he licks icing off his lips or flicks his hair out of his eyes. And he needs to touch me, like always."

"What does this perfect man look like?"

She yawned again. "He must have your eyes, Oli. You have beautiful eyes."

His breath caught, and he tightened his grip on his phone. "I do? They're just hazel."

"Nope," she sang. "They change between green, brown, and gray depending on your mood or what you wear."

Something snapped open, and she yelped, "Gloves," then running water followed. "What does your woman look like, Oli?"

His woman? He frowned. Oh, yes, his unrequited love. "Curvaceous, big blue eyes, curly black hair, and an olive skin tone. Her smile lights up her face and the room." He held his breath. Would Navy recognize herself in the description?

"She sounds amazing. Alas, she's also an idiot, Oli. She should be begging you to take her." Navy giggled. "Oh, I like that." The thump-thump of bare feet on a hardwood floor preceded the squeal of chair wheels. "Writing that down before I make the nipples."

"Nipples?" he groaned.

"Yup." She yawned. "I'm making burlesque cupcakes for a bridal shower. The nipples are cherries dipped in chocolate."

He squeezed his eyes shut. "Might want to add that as foreplay."

"Huh?"

Despite clearing his throat, his voice rasped. "Slather your character's nipples in warm chocolate."

Navy gasped. "And he sucks…" The rapid tapping on a keyboard drowned her words. Something dinged in the background. The typing stopped. "Got to dip those nipples. Thanks for calling, and if you come home, I'll treat you to dessert too. Kisses!"

He blinked at his phone long after the call had ended. This was going to be the death of him. He slid his phone on the nightstand and thumped his pillow. *If* he came home? She had no idea.

He snorted. Neither did he. Even Google was elusive on how to woo her. Fuck, he needed a game plan and fast.

~*~

"It looks like a penis." Tina frowned while sipping her morning coffee. "Maybe add more balls?"

With exhaustion burning behind her eyes, Navy studied her midnight cake creation and giggled. Yes, she could see it now. "It's a rocket, and those balls are smoke plumes." She sighed as she stenciled small circles out of a single layer of chocolate cake and added it to the bottom. "Better?"

"Now it's alien porn," Tina laughed. "I thought you wrote contemporary romance."

"I do," Navy huffed. "And no, sex isn't on every damn page."

"Well, girl, you need some."

Navy studied her creation, trying to find the missing element. "What?"

"Sex."

"Me?" Navy squealed, slapped her chest with a gloved hand and sprayed cake crumbs everywhere. "I'm not the one seeing phallic symbols in my baking."

Tina arched a brow and pointed with her coffee mug at the side counter that held four dozen pale caramel fondant cupcakes with dark brown cherries on them. Navy had dipped the cherries in chocolate and placed them centerstage. Memories of Oli telling her what to do with her character's nipples froze her breath in her chest and exploded a cloud of powdered sugar in her belly. Wow, the man was lethal. It was such a pity he loved someone else.

Wait? What? This was Oli, her brother's best friend. Thinking of him in a sexual way was O.U.T. He was family. Still, the way his voice had deepened, rasping across her ears, almost guttural, stirred heat within her. Must be exhaustion addling her mind.

"Hey, those are for Nanette's bridal shower." She lowered her chin to hide her warm cheeks. "They asked for nipples."

"They said ni*bb*les." Tina enunciated the double 'b.'

"The art of baking is a sensual act," Navy muttered. "I'm adding lace detailing so it looks like breasts encased in lingerie." Okay, so maybe she'd misinterpreted the brief, but still, they'd look gorgeous when she was done. Her trip into the valley of erotica baking had nothing to do with Oli's call.

Oh, sugar, he had a sexy voice. Her man, wherever the hell he was, had to have the same and the balls to ask her out. None of this does-he-doesn't-he B.S.

She glanced at the photo on the fridge—Oli, Gray, and herself as teenagers. Oli's blond hair flopped over his temple, his more-gray-than-green eyes gazed into the camera. He'd thrown his arm across her shoulders. Minutes before the photo was taken, they'd elbowed each other in the ribs, intermittent with tickles. His eyes had sparkled, his smile had been broad, and carefree laughter had rumbled up from his belly. Why hadn't she developed a crush on him?

Ah. She gritted her teeth. Because of Ronnie Landon. He'd been about to kiss her at her sixteenth birthday party. She was on the verge of realizing her dreams, snagging the high school jock. Ronnie with his bright smile, dark hair and eyes had every girl in school swooning, Navy included.

Oli had stormed into her room, glared at Ronnie's hand on her bare knee, and tossed him out of her room. "This is how you honor your parents' trust...?" He'd dragged his gaze over her body, his lips curling in derision. "And what the hell are you wearing, Blue? You look like the school slut."

She'd gasped, glanced at her denim mini skirt and pink tank top, and punched him like he'd taught her. The satisfying crack was his nose breaking. She hadn't given a shit. Not an ounce of remorse had swept through her.

Like the child she'd been, she hadn't spoken a word to him until his mom's funeral. Ronnie hadn't looked at her again, especially after he knocked up Jenny Stanton and had to marry her. Now they had *the* perfect life. A beautiful house, the two-point-four children, and here was Navy, alone, childless.

In hindsight, Oli had been right to chastise her, to protect her honor. She should've expected no less from him. As a teenager, being horribly embarrassed at her birthday party, having her dreams crushed, and her heart broken... He could've handled it better.

Still, he'd had her best interests at heart. He'd cared far more than Gray ever had.

He cared now to endure her pestering him at all hours of the morning.

She sighed, trying to marry her lingering anger with her adoration for her oldest friend. One would think, after a decade, she might be able to forgive and forget. But every time she saw the Landons, a knife twisted in her gut along with the words, '*that could have been me.*'

"What's ready to go?" Tina slid her finger along the edge of an empty bowl of icing sugar, popping the dollop into her mouth.

"Let me finish icing the plumes of smoke, then that can go. Milly's bread and pies are in the crates, and while you're out delivering the wedding cake..." She glanced at the tower of white on her dining room table. Flowers in silver and lilac spiraled around the three tiers of white fondant. "I'll lace the cupcakes."

"Holy shit, Navy. I can't believe you did it all." Tina spun in a slow circle. "Okay, I'll do the wedding cake first, since that will take the longest. Lemme call Lisa to help me load it into the van." She pinned her phone between shoulder and ear as she stacked crates by the front door.

Navy scanned the crowded counter for her coffee, ice-cold by now. Finding it, she threw it back and prayed the caffeine kicked in soon. While Tina loaded the van with Milly's order, Navy mixed a small batch of white icing sugar and, with sweeps of a butter knife, created wisps of clouds on the newly added balls to the rocket. She leaned back and smiled. Better. A last sprinkle of silver edible stars finished it off. She slipped it into a box and sealed it, writing Kevin's name on the top.

Now for the fun part. Adding black food coloring to white chocolate, she stirred it over low heat, then poured the mixture into a piping bag. She could flatten the chocolate and use a stencil, but because of the dome shape of the cupcake, it would be quicker to do the lace detailing by hand.

With flicks of her wrist, she drew scalloped edges across and over the cherry, then filled in the bottom half of the cupcake with dots and flowers. And so on, until four dozen were done. Her wrist burned from the repetitive motion, but all she could do was shake her hand. She was too tired to take the time to R.I.C.E. it. After packing them into crates, she sprawled onto her three-seater couch and was asleep before her head hit the armrest.

Chapter Three

Navy awoke with a jerk. She frowned, trying to get her bearings. Sitting up, she scanned the kitchen. It was a mess. Stands to reason after the miracle she'd performed through the night. Tina had taken everything but the cupcakes. Navy glanced at the time. Two o'clock? Sugarplums, that wouldn't do, not when the party started in two hours. She hurried down the short passage and into the en suite to take a shower then brush her teeth. In a fresh pair of jeans and a long-sleeved T-shirt, she hopped on each foot, stamping on the boots.

Hefting a crate, she stepped through her front door and yelped. It had snowed heavily which might be why Tina had yet to finish all the deliveries, especially if Jim's plow was down again. After a few back and forth trips, Navy had the crates strapped to her snow machine. With her trusty scarf and hideously rainbow-striped woolen hat, she careened out of the driveway.

And into a red SUV.

She squealed and veered the snow machine at the last minute, tilting it and almost flipping it onto its side. Fighting the momentum, she managed to settle the machine onto its tracks, then leapt off it to lambaste the asshat who'd driven his vehicle into the ditch.

Her words lodged in her throat at the man sliding out of his SUV. Holy sugar, he was gorgeous, all broad shoulders, massive hands, and legs that went on for days. His jeans molded to his sculpted thighs and ass. And when he settled his hazel gaze on her, the fury in them flushed her face to the tips of her ears. He circled to the front of the SUV where it was wedged into the ditch.

She gathered her anger, drew her scattered wits together, and glanced at her crates. A shiver tore through her, and she gasped, lunging for the top crate. "My nipples!"

"Your what?"

Ignoring him, she crouched next to the snow machine, wincing at the smear of black chocolate along the inside of the crate. "Of all the..." She stomped across to the offender, rested her hands on her hips, and shoved her face in his. In her sexy stilettos, she'd reach his chin. Now, in her military boots, she reached his Adam's apple. "Look what you did. They're ruined." She poked him in the chest, wincing when her finger hit solid muscle.

"Me?" His voice was deep, dark, hoarse—the stuff of fantasies. "There's no warning for the road's abrupt end."

She huffed. Yup, something she raised at the last town meeting, but alas, to no avail. She threw her hands in the air when he blinked at her, fluttering the longest eyelashes. While pinching her lips, she studied the line of his nose—broken at some point. There was something familiar about him.

"There's the sign... So tiny, you'd need eagle eyes to read it." She gestured to the sign covered in snow.

He peered over her head, blessing her with a lovely view of his angular jaw, the dimple in his squarish chin, and the long column of his neck, laced with intriguing tattoos. "I'll be damned."

"You're double-damned, mister. The snowplow's probably broken, which means getting the tow truck here will be tricky." She stumbled back and twisted to study the damage. "The bumper's bad." She briefly closed her eyes at her 'expert' opinion. "You'll have to come with me." Hitching a thumb at her home not fifty yards away, she ogled him some more when he raised his gaze to study her ranch-style house. "I'll call Harry and see if he can help you." She tugged her phone out of her pocket and dialed.

Turning her back on the stranger, she unclipped the top crate's lid. One row had collided with the side, smudging the lace. The rest were fine. She released a whoosh. Baker's dozen had saved her ass more times than she could count.

"Hey, Tina, please collect then deliver Nanette's cupcakes. I had an accident."

"What?" Tina squeaked and whispered something to Lisa.

"I'm fine, just have..." Navy glanced at her 'guest,' "...company. I'll leave the snow machine at the top of the driveway."

"Sure thing, boss."

"And enjoy your trip. See you in nine days." Navy hung up and dialed Sheriff Harry Martin. "Hey, bestie." She chuckled. The man was in no way her best friend, but she loved to tweak his non-existent goatee.

"What do you want, Navy?"

She settled her gaze on her guest. "Got another idiot almost colliding with the barrier. I swear I warned you—"

"Yeah, I heard you. One every six months isn't a hazard, Navy." Cheering pierced her ears, and she yanked her phone away. "I can't come through now. All officers are at the Shoot and Toot. I'll drop by later, snow permitting."

"But—" She growled when he hung up. Right. Shooting competitions between towns mattered more than any inconvenience this caused her. Shoving her phone into her pocket, she approached the stranger. "Sheriff's busy. Said he'll stop by later." She leaned her ample ass on the snow machine's seat and grinned when the stranger stomped to the rear of his SUV.

He hauled his luggage out and marched toward her. She swung her leg over the seat and patted behind her, tossing him a smirk as if to say 'come on, big boy.' When he straddled the snow machine with his long legs, his easy movement dampened her good humor. He was such a show-off. But she couldn't stew on it when he snuggled his chest against her back and looped his arm across her belly. He hung his luggage over his shoulder by a hooked finger.

His cologne engulfed her; a spicy fragrance summoning images of cherry-flavored cigars and cinnamon incense. She was left with no doubt he was all male. Sighing, she started the snow machine and drove the short distance to her sprawling house.

Despite the style not suited to this weather and her pocket, she'd loved it on sight. Since she didn't entertain often, the living room with its massive fireplace was in a decent condition, and she'd dusted three days ago.

It was her bakery-kitchen she worried about. Chaos from her all-nighter dominated every surface. There was nothing to be done about it. She jerked the snow machine to a halt and twisted to meet the man's penetrating gaze. "Well, are you getting off?"

He did with ease but not before giving her a squeeze. Frowning, she bit her lip, not wanting to read anything into that overly casual gesture. She hopped off the snow machine, left the keys in the ignition, and led the way into her home.

"Sorry about the mess. I had to work late." She unraveled her scarf, ripped her woolen cap off her head, and hung them on the hooks provided. After gesturing to the large, leather couches, she darted behind the massive island, grabbing pans and bowls as she hurried past. "Coffee?"

"Please." He placed his luggage in the hallway and slid off his jacket, revealing a forest-green, long-sleeved T-shirt clinging to an impressive chest. Striding across her living room, he settled onto the double seater, folded his long legs, and faced her, elbows on his knees, hands clasped between them.

His gaze trailed her as she brewed fresh coffee and cleaned up, working on each counter until order reigned.

His eyes twinkled. "Outside you said 'nipples?'" Having assumed nothing could make his mouth sexier, when his lips twitched, she blinked at him like a virgin at a BDSM club.

"Yeah, my masterpieces for a bridal shower. I'm a baker." She dipped her chin as she set out mugs, sugar, cream, and the prototype for the nipple idea. "Baking bread is dull, so when I get the chance, I try out new things. The folks of Colefield have been so supportive." After pouring black liquid gold into each mug, she carried the tray to the coffee table.

He studied her, not the tray, nor her nipple-black-lace creation. "You don't recognize me, do you?"

She shrugged. "You do look familiar."

He laughed. "This scenario never occurred to me. And I don't know how I feel about you inviting a stranger into your home, Blue."

"Blue?" She studied him again and settled on the same nose she'd broken. No, it couldn't be. Tears burned the backs of her eyes—she blamed exhaustion for her weakness. "Oli?" Her voice cracked.

He grinned, his smile dominating his face. Her heart leapt to choke her, and she threw herself at him. He caught her and yanked her onto his lap, his embrace meaning more to her than a thousand wedding cakes.

"I can't believe it," she sniffed, leaned back, and met his gaze while wiping tears off her cheeks. "You came."

"I said I would." He smiled, and when he rubbed her back, she melted into a blubbering mess. "Don't cry, Blue." He cradled her against him, tucking her head under his chin.

"You and Gray have been promising for years." She stilled. "Is Gray coming too? No. Don't' answer. I'd rather he surprise me *if* he visits." She tried to scramble off Oli's lap, but he held firm. "Sorry, I forgot you don't like hugs."

"I was a teenager lacking control of my body." He kissed her temple. The brush of his lips across her skin stole her breath. "Hug away."

She was helpless to stop him from tightening his arms, and she didn't want to. "You're staying with me, right?" She snuggled deeper.

He stilled, ceasing to rub her back. "If the offer stands."

"Oh, Oli, it will be wonderful having you home." She wiggled on his lap to cup his jaw. "How long are you staying? Want to visit my mom with me?" She shook her head. Here she was taking over his visit. He might have other plans.

"Of course. I'd love to see your mom."

She gasped. Right then, she adored him. "You would?"

His hazel eyes swirled to gray, mesmerizing her. "Yes."

She dashed away another tear and slid off his lap. "Come, let's have coffee before it gets cold…and a nipple…I mean, cupcake." While he poured sugar and cream into his coffee, she dialed the butcher. "Ray, I need a pound of elk meat delivered."

"What are you making, Navy? Elk Shepherd's Pie?" He hummed amid the repetitive thwack of a butcher's knife in the background.

She laughed, picturing skinny-as-hell Ray rubbing his flat stomach. "Yup, as soon as possible." She settled her gaze on Oli, who twirled the cupcake plate, studying her creation.

"I'll have Pete drop it off tomorrow morning."

She flicked her gaze at the afternoon sunlight. Tomorrow would have to do. "Perfect, thanks." After hanging up, she fixed her coffee, sat on the opposite side of the couch, but faced Oli.

"This looks better than I imagined." He tore off the nipple and popped it into his mouth, his eyelids fluttering closed on a groan. "Maraschino?"

She nodded while squeezing her thighs together. When the hell had Oli become this sexy? Holy sugarplums, her lady bits were having a fiesta.

He bit into the cupcake and stilled, his gaze settling on her. His nostrils flared, and she froze, dreading his reaction. Heat swirled in his eyes. He swallowed, his Adam's apple bobbed, then he swiped the caramel off his top lip with his thumb before licking it off.

She shifted, finding the intense burn between her legs distracting. She shivered. Reacting like this to folks' appreciation was new. Shit, she hoped this didn't happen often.

"You like?" She forced a smile. Baking and writing had similar rewards when the consumers of both gushed their appreciation. It sent tingles from her belly to her soul and fueled her to write more, bake more.

"Fuck, Blue, this is…" He squeezed his eyes shut then met her gaze. "Heaven. The chocolate is moist, but the dollop of caramel in the center acts as an explosion of smoky sweetness. And there are hints of something more, maybe roses?"

She beamed. "Turkish delight."

He took another bite, humming as he did so. Another shiver threatened to sweep over her; one she struggled to suppress. The way he devoured the cupcake meant his compliments were sincere. It mattered what he thought. It always had even after he'd stepped between her and Ronnie. Ignoring him had been a duel-edged sword. He'd been the one she'd confided in when things became difficult after Dad died and Mom spiraled downhill with Alzheimer's. Sure, Gray paid for Mom's retirement, but he never visited. He'd done so once, and when Mom had asked him who he was, it had broken his heart.

Navy sipped her coffee, content to watch Oli suck the caramel off his thumb.

"You're wasted in Colefield, sweetheart."

She shrugged. "This is my home, Oli. Being another unknown in a massive city? No, thanks. I like that the Greens have an argument every Christmas. I like that Nancy Alvarez tries to stab her sister at least once a year. I love that Maude Olson is having a wild affair."

Oli gaped. "What? But she's—"

"Eighty." Navy giggled. "What I don't like is that they're up in your business when you like someone."

Oli stilled. "Who do you like, Blue?"

"No one. He doesn't matter." She flicked a hand but pinched her lips. Chasing after an asshole who couldn't even ask her out? Pointless. But she was stubborn. She'd continue to deliver cupcakes and not spare Antony another glance.

"Navy?" Oli arched a brow. "Does he have eyes like mine?"

She laughed. "Nope. So, no one to worry about. I just thought he was cute, y'know. It's been three months and nothing, not an inkling of interest." She slid her coffee onto the table. "Let's get you settled."

Leaping to her feet, she slammed into Oli who'd done the same. He caught her, steadying her with a firm grip on her hip. She was so close, her nose was an inch from his chest. The air thickened, her senses heightened, and she raised her gaze to his. What the hell was going on?

Chapter Four

From the moment Navy climbed off the snow machine, stomped toward him with her dark curls across her face, and her finger jabbed at his chest, Oliver had known he was a goner. Air stuck in his lungs as he drank in the sight of her. In four years, she'd grown more beautiful, filled out into wider curves, more sensual than he'd dreamed. She was a bundle of fiery energy, her gaze bold, fearless, and her blue eyes as beautiful as he remembered.

Cuddling her on the snow machine had been a low and high point for him. She hadn't realized who he was, so to her, he was a stranger sneaking in a feel. Fuck, but she smelled so good, and after eating her cupcake—and no, that wasn't a euphemism—he knew why. Vanilla, sugar, and lavender surrounded her. *When* she was his, he would breathe her scent into his lungs...daily.

And her baking... It was an orgasm in his mouth—no, not a euphemism either. The explosion of flavors, bold and subtle were indicative of the woman pouring love into her creations.

She'd let him hug her, but when she cried in his arms, what lingering doubts he'd had evaporated. This was Navy, the woman who'd conquered his heart without trying. To get it back, no amount of effort would be wasted. Losing himself in her blue eyes, he rubbed her arms then slid his hands along her shoulders to cup her neck. With his thumbs positioned under her jaw, he tilted her face to admire the silkiness of her skin, the pink glow on her cheeks, and the sexiest mouth he'd ever seen. All it would take was a dip of his head. He could kiss her, taste those lips, yet he hesitated, too scared to risk their relationship.

"I'm glad you're home," she whispered.

With a pat on his chest, she pulled away and strolled down the passage, pausing outside a door on the left. Flicking on the lights, she gestured to him to enter while she hurried to the hall closet to grab linen. He lowered his bag then captured the end of the fitted sheet, helping her tuck it in.

"Do you think you're too big?" She studied the double bed then him, running her gaze over his legs.

He grinned. "Women haven't complained before."

"Oh!" She blushed that pretty pink again. Her laughter bubbled over and bounced off the walls.

He threw himself onto the bed and stretched, folding his arms behind his head to wink at her. "Think I fit? Nothing I can do to change my size, gorgeous. You'll just have to accept that."

Giggling, she sprawled alongside him, resting her head on his arm. "I'm not worried, and besides, you're not staying long."

He flipped onto his side, threw his arm over her waist, and tickled her like he used to do when they watched movies on Christmas Eve while their parents sat on the porch. Gray would be elbows deep in the popcorn bowl, fixed on the movie, moaning at them whenever they bumped him.

"Oh, no, you don't," she squealed, climbing on top of Oliver and pinning him to the bed. "I'm bigger now too."

He relished the moment, her thighs spread wide as she straddled his hips, her delicate hands pressed his shoulders, and tumbling dark curls cast her face into shadow.

"Still a weakling," he chuckled, rolling her over until he trapped her beneath him.

"Oli," she cried out, squirming as if she could wriggle free.

His breath caught, and he captured her face between his hands, stroking her skin with his thumbs. She stilled, her eyes twinkling, her breathing ragged. The ache to kiss her barreled over him. He slid his arms underneath her and hugged her, burying his face in her hair and the pillow.

She wrapped her arms around him, and where she touched, his skin tingled beneath her fingers.

"I've missed you…this, Blue," he confessed.

She huffed. "Missed means regular visits."

"That goes both ways, sweetheart." He leaned back to grin at her.

She blinked at him and blessed him with a languorous smile. "You're right. I'm sorry. I never thought of driving through to the city. Are you getting off me anytime soon?"

He pouted. "Do I have to?"

"Oh, Oli, that's adorable." She thrummed his bottom lip like a kalimba.

"Fine, don't take me seriously." He climbed off her, then nudged her playfully. "Quit fooling around, woman. We need to make my bed."

"Me?" she squeaked and slapped his arm but hopped off the bed to straighten the sheet. "What do you want to do tonight? Or do you have plans?"

"Yes, I have a date…with you, pizza, TV, and a roaring fire."

"Sounds wonderful." She sighed. "I could sleep for days."

"We'll start early then. Three kinds of cheese with olives, right?" He worked the pillow into a case, fluffed and placed it.

She nodded while stuffing the duvet inner inside the cover. "You don't care as long as it has bacon."

He grinned. "Damn straight, Blue. Let's ditch the olives and add the bacon."

"Works for me." She flicked the duvet and tucked it in, gesturing to him to do his side. "Want to shower or anything while I order?"

"If you don't mind?" A strategy was beginning to form. At fucking last.

He could try bombarding her with his presence but in subtle ways. He smothered a snort. Then it wouldn't be a bombardment. Like a woman when she wanted to entice her man; show more skin, smell good, sexy lingerie… He chuckled, earning a glance from Navy for his silliness. Women just had to flash cleavage, didn't they know that?

He glanced at his jeans and shirt. "We'll hop into our pajamas and spend the night on the couch like it's Christmas Eve."

She gasped and raised wide eyes to meet his gaze. "Can we?"

She was too adorable. There had to be a cuteness meter out there. Regardless, she was off the charts.

He smiled. "Sure, Blue."

She bolted for his en suite, hung towels, and skipped out of his room, closing the door behind her. As he unpacked his bag, he mused over her belief he wouldn't be staying long. What would she say or do when she learned the truth? Fuck, what would he do if she rejected him? If this quest to win her heart was an unmitigated failure? Could he live knowing she was in the arms of another man?

He gritted his teeth, hating the twinge of fire burning from his chest to the pit of his stomach. Part of him wanted her to be happy. The other selfish part wanted her to be happy *with him*. Still, should things head downhill, if he ran back to the city with his tail between his legs, Pops could manage on his own.

Oliver stripped, dumping his clothes in the hamper. While planning the next steps, he lathered and rinsed. First, a subtle seduction. Gentle touches, hopefully showing her he was more than her oldest friend. And he wanted her to realize how good they were together. He hadn't been this relaxed in a woman's company in years.

While drying himself off, he smiled at the gray yoga pants he draped across the bed. Research had shown women found the pants appealing. Well, he would soon find out. He pulled them on. Their low-hanging waistband was comfortable, and the way the fabric draped over his cock flattered him. He studied himself in the mirror and grinned. All those hours in the gym showed in the Adonis belt peeking above the waistband. Slipping a white T-shirt on that highlighted his broad shoulders, bulging biceps, and firm pecs was the icing on the cake. After the slightest spritz of his cologne, he grabbed a towel and padded barefoot to the kitchen while rubbing his hair dry.

With his gaze fixed on Navy, he waited for her reaction but tried not to look like he watched her. A fire crackled in the massive fireplace beneath the big screen TV mounted above the mantelpiece.

Christmas carols played. He chuckled. "Good choice of music."

She faced him with a bag of marshmallows in her hand. Her eyes widened, her cheeks bloomed, and she parted her luscious mouth on a gasp. She shivered. He couldn't have asked for better reactions. Well, maybe her throwing herself into his arms and kissing him?

"Won't you be cold in that?" she squeaked, and with trembling fingers, placed the marshmallows on the counter.

"We have a fire, a blanket, and body heat." He shrugged.

"Those tattoos are stunning, Oli." She crossed to him, caught his wrist, and ran her fingers up the geometric-tribal patterns with letters hidden in the design. If she looked carefully, she'd see her name. He held his breath as she stroked him, trailing a path up to his shoulder and neck.

Willing himself to slow his breathing without her noticing, he hitched his thumb at her bedroom. "I'll listen for the pizza. You change."

She glanced at her T-shirt. He followed her gaze and lingered on her taut nipples tenting the fabric. After she disappeared down the hallway, he waited until she closed her bedroom door. Then with a silent whoop, he did a little dance. Score one to him.

He straightened the couch, chose the softest blanket from the ones she'd rolled into a woven basket, and stoked the flames of the fire. He withdrew cash from his wallet and left it on the side table, then dimmed the lights. As soon as the knock came, he whipped the front door open, shivered at the blast of frigid air, shoved the money at the delivery man, and with pizza in hand, snapped the door closed.

With the savory aroma rising from the pizza on the coffee table, he settled on the couch, taking calming breaths while he waited for her.

"Blue, the hot cocoa is getting cold," he called.

"I'm here," she rasped, hurrying into the living room in leggings and a fleecy top. Her hair glistened like melted licorice so she must have showered too. She climbed onto the couch beside him, still rubbing lavender-scented lotion on her arms.

Reaching across her, he tucked the blanket around her, then pulled the pizza box onto their laps. "What do you want to watch?" He flipped the box open and offered her a slice.

"Mm," she moaned around a bite. "You choose."

"Something with action?" He wiggled his eyebrows while looping an arm around her to tug her into the curve of his body.

"Typical," she mumbled. "There better be a romance arc in it."

"Fair enough." He flicked through the channels until something exploded on the screen. Settling deeper into the couch, he drew her closer and grabbed a slice of pizza. "This is the life, Blue."

"Sure is." She snuggled against him and rested her head on his chest.

It wasn't long before her breathing deepened and her hand holding a half-eaten slice of pizza sagged. She *had* worked through the night, and despite her falling asleep on him, he cherished her company. Rescuing the pizza from her, he slid the box onto the coffee table and wrapped his arms around her.

While the movie played in the background and the fire crackled in the hearth, he pressed a kiss to her temple and imagined this was his life, his future. With Navy nestled against his chest, her scent saturating his senses, he'd never been happier.

Chapter Five

Navy surfaced, her face smashed against something firm yet giving and smelling incredible. She rubbed her nose across it, drawing in the spicy mix of cinnamon and man. Her eyes flew open to the delicious vision of a sleeping Oli. Yesterday, he'd been amazing. She'd felt like a kid again, carefree and among family and friends.

She stilled her twitching fingers stroking his tattoo. Holy sugar, he was a sexy man in his yoga pants and T-shirt. She'd damn near swallowed her tongue when he'd strolled into the kitchen, still damp from a shower. *Wow.* Her cheeks flared as she relived that moment. She dipped her temple, resting it on a pec. She had no right to think of him in that way. Maybe Tina had guessed it. Maybe Navy was sex-starved?

He shifted and mumbled, "My love."

She gasped, unable to grant him privacy when she was trapped in his tight embrace. If she hadn't hesitated, she wouldn't be in this situation. Gaping at him, she refused to blink. What if he thought she was his unrequited?

A squeal lodged in her throat.

When he did nothing except put her senses on high alert, she relaxed. Now to escape. But being held against his chest wasn't unpleasant. She huffed. Who was she kidding? It was amazing. She snuggled deeper despite her inner voice urging her to wiggle free and bolt for her room. When he'd hugged his 'my love,' he'd shifted Navy higher. She could bury her face in the curve of his neck and breathe in his delicious cologne. Doing so now, she succumbed and rubbed her nose along the column of his throat.

He squeezed her, sparking a pang of guilt. No, he was her dearest friend. Tears burned at the backs of her eyes. If only.

"Sweetheart, what's wrong?" His sleep-drenched voice, hoarse, so epically masculine, pierced her longing.

Oh, sugar. Had he caught her sniffing him?

He relaxed an arm, and that precious moment where she mattered to someone was lost. Despair was swift to strike, but she didn't dare sniffle lest he awoke and flicked aside the tear slipping free.

He pinched her chin between forefinger and thumb and urged her to meet his hooded gaze. She tried to fight him, but he held firm. *Oh, sugarplums, no.* But resisting him was futile, so she squeezed her eyes shut.

At a soft grunt, he brushed his mouth across hers.

She froze. *No fridging way.* Her over-romantic mind must have imagined it.

Don't move, Navy. He's dreaming.

Her breath tangled in her throat at the thought of him waking up with his lips on hers. The potential embarrassment alone set off her inner squeal...again.

He released her chin and dragged his knuckles down her throat, resting his thumb in the hollow of her collarbone. Goosebumps skittered outward. Morning breath be damned. She was taking this gift and cherishing it. She parted her lips, relishing the heat of the man beneath her.

Before she could scramble off him, rethink her lust-induced actions, and somehow end this insanity, he swept his tongue across her bottom lip then delved into her mouth. He crushed her against him, bombarding her on many fronts. His cologne, his hard body, his hands splaying across her back, and his hot tongue plunging in, dominating her senses and thoughts.

He broke the kiss, his breathing ragged. Then he lay there, not loosening his hold, his eyes closed as he rested his temple on hers. "Sleep, my love."

She pretended to obey, shifting to press her cheek to his chest. His arms relaxed as sleep claimed him, but there was nowhere on a wedding cake she'd stay where she was. What if he tempted fate and kissed her again? What if he realized what he was doing and with whom?

She couldn't chance it.

Minutes ticked by, his erratic heartbeat calmed, and with the warmth of him drenching her, she snoozed. Jerking herself awake, she listened, rising to study his face. *Go for it, Navy. Don't wait. Be quick.*

She slithered off him and the couch, to the rug, then crawled into the kitchen. Grabbing onto the counter, she pulled herself up, inch by inch, her gaze fixed on his prostate figure illuminated by the dying fire.

He hadn't moved.

She bolted for her room, clicking the door shut, then the bathroom door, to sit on the edge of the bathtub and rub her throbbing knees. Her heartbeat pounded in her ears. Goosebumps did the Mexican wave across her skin, and she trembled like a battered pinata. But she couldn't say if it was from running or Oli's kiss.

Her nipples tingled, but worse than this was the growing ache in her core; hot and demanding. Oh no, she wanted Oli, as in sexually. Holy sugar, how was she going to hide this from him? How could she pretend all was the same? And the poor man had done nothing wrong.

What if...she focused on Antony? If she channeled this madness into pursuing him? Not that it was fair on him when she desired another, but maybe what she was feeling was just desire in general?

Splashing water onto her face, she studied her reflection: flushed cheeks, kiss-swollen lips, wide eyes darkened with a hint of panic jarring her breathing. "Get a grip, Navy. He won't remember in the morning."

She nodded but didn't lower her gaze while drying her face. The small digital clock on the vanity said it was four AM. Going to sleep when her body buzzed didn't seem likely. She left the bathroom and cracked open her bedroom door, then hurried down the hallway and into her study. Sealing herself inside, she switched on the laptop and sank into the office chair. She scrolled to the scene where Roman almost kissed Hannah.

"Just once, y'know, I'd like to be in a situation where the hero urgently kisses the heroine." Hannah gestured to the flatscreen TV. "Look at them. He's about to leave her, head into danger to disarm a bomb, and yet, kissing her is a priority."

"I don't know. Maybe he's thinking he's going to die, and he might as well kiss her?" Roman stretched out his long legs, resting his sock-covered feet on the coffee table.

"True, but still..." She slumped, snuggling deeper into the couch. "I write about it but lack the experience. The last time a man kissed me, he asked first. Sure, that can be romantic..."

She snuck a glance at Roman and stilled. He stared at her, his brown eyes hooded, intense, like he was deep in thought. "What do you do? Ask?"

"Sometimes."

Right, a one-word answer. She could so use his expertise.

Navy paused. Like she had done with Oli. His input was paramount to her novels.

He folded his legs and shifted closer to cup her jaw, urging her to face him. "Which is preferable? Taking or asking first? What if the kiss isn't wanted?"

She angled her body toward him, forcing him to lower his hand. His unexpected caress jolted her heart—an electric shock that made no sense. Not when he wasn't into her like that. "There has to be some behavioral markers, Roman. Charged air between them, sparks when they touch, their gazes focusing on lips."

His laughter was rich, and like a double chocolate chip cookie, made her all gooey inside. "Only in romance novels, sweetheart."

She gaped. "What? No sparks?" Harumphing, she folded her arms across her pebbled nipples, having enjoyed his touch too much.

Navy's alarm went off, set to six even on weekends. She hadn't changed much in *Hounding Hannah*, but at least her body wasn't thrumming with desire. Stretching, she worked the kinks from her back, tilting her head to listen when sounds emanated from the kitchen.

Oli was awake.

Her heart leapt again. She tamped down her excitement. Acting normal was the goal, and her body overreacting wouldn't help. Opening her mailbox, she went through author mails from her social media platforms, various beta readers, and her editor. Then closing that, she browsed the bakery's mails and orders, settling bills, and restocking depleted ingredients.

The tap on the door drew a squeak and snapped her from a daze. She'd been staring at the cover of *Hounding Hannah*. "Come in." Clutching the edge of the wraparound counter that served as her workspace, she forced herself not to touch her hair or straighten her top.

Oli's smile was the first thing she zeroed on. Fridging stunning, all charming, sensual, and dominating his face. Those lips had been on hers. Then the aroma of coffee greeted her, and she smiled at the tray in his hands.

"Good morning. How did you sleep?" He slid the tray onto an empty spot and pulled up a chair.

In his yoga pants and white T-shirt, his presence dwarfed the confined space. The striking design of his tattoo made her want to rip off his shirt and trace the dark etchings with her lips. Her body arched toward him, as if he could soothe *whatever* ailed her. She rolled her eyes. Like she had no idea? Lust played pinball with her ovaries.

"Well, thank you. I can't imagine the couch was comfortable. But you slept so deeply, I didn't have the heart to wake you."

His gaze settled on the laptop screen. "Hounding Hannah?"

"Yeah, I'm rewriting a few scenes." She clicked on the bookmark which took her to the latest edited section.

He narrowed his eyes, jerked back, and settled his gaze on her. "But I love this scene. Where he pins her to the wall..."

Right then, she double-adored Oli. He was her biggest fan, and she hadn't realized how much that mattered. "I thought it lacked...something. Tension?"

"Hell no, it's perfect. I highlighted it and often reread..." He lowered his gaze, his cheeks darkening. "I don't mean to gush."

The chair squeaked when she lunged to capture his fingers gripping his knee. "Thank you for your support, Oli. I can't tell you how much it means to me."

He flipped his hand over and caught hers, then before she could snatch it back, he lifted it to his lips. Sparks rippled up her arm from where he brushed a kiss across her knuckles. "Anything for you, Blue. Now, show me what you've changed?" He released her hand and rose, forcing her to face her laptop.

When she did so, he grasped her shoulders, swirling his thumbs across tense muscles. She tried to stifle a moan, but it felt incredible. He kissed the crown of her head as he massaged her. Swallowing past the lump in her throat, she scrolled to the beginning of the scene.

"Just tweaking, to be honest. I don't think editing is ever finished, even after a novel's published." She twisted to meet his gaze. The change in position placed his hands at the base of her throat. His touch softened to a caress. "Was thinking of writing a series. Titillating Typists? Alluring Annotators?" She huffed. "I'll think of a title later."

He stroked her collarbone, then gripped her upper arms before releasing her. "That's brilliant. How many do you plan to write for the series?" He shifted to the side and fixed her coffee, adding just the right amount of cream and sugar.

"It's up in the air. As and when a story idea comes to mind." She smiled her thanks when he slid the coffee across the desk to her. "Y'know, sometimes I think I write because I lack love in my life. Tina believes I'm sex-starved and writing out my fantasies." *Now why did I say that?* She sipped her coffee to hide the blush warming her face from chin to ears.

The teaspoon clattered when it bounced off his mug. "Maybe." His voice was hoarse, but he cleared his throat and resumed his seat. "Planning on testing that theory?" He stirred his coffee, his gaze fixed on the spoon.

"With whom? The only guy kind of decent is Antony."

Oli stilled with the mug midway to his mouth. "Who?"

"The cute guy I mentioned. He's a fireman I've been batting my eyelashes at. Hell, I could smear icing sugar on my nipples and do the Can-Can naked, and he wouldn't notice."

Oli's gaze dipped to her chest. As if his interest was tied to her core, her breasts tingled. "Maybe he's shy? Did you ask him on a date?"

She harumphed. Tina and Oli must have exchanged notes. "He was an inch from me yesterday and didn't 'accidentally' touch me. And no, every time I open my mouth to ask him, nonsense comes out. Just watching me around him, you wouldn't believe I'm an author with an extensive vocabulary."

Oli hummed, sipped his coffee, then clasped the mug between his parted thighs. She couldn't help but linger on a nicely defined package in his clingy yoga pants. Well, linger was mild. She damn well ogled. *Sugar-honey-ice-tea, look anywhere but there, Navy!* She settled on his hands. Long fingers, wide palms, with a dusting of blond hair along his forearms. At what he could do with said hands, her mind went there in graphic detail. A shiver shuddered her shoulders and slithered heat down her spine to her pelvis. *Right, don't look there either.* She fixed her gaze on his face, then clenched her thighs when he licked his bottom lip after sipping coffee. Those lips had been on hers. Her breath hitched, so she stared at her hands as she rubbed her thighs to her knees and up again.

"Let me give this some thought."

"What?" She frowned. "Why?"

A slow smile crawled across his sensual mouth. "Flirting sometimes requires strategy, especially if your emotions are involved and you're desperate for victory."

She shook her head. "I don't know him well enough for me to like or love him. But if he wanted to, he could've asked me, Oli. I got nothing, nada."

"Is Max still the chief?" When she nodded, he continued, "Might have to stop by, y'know, since he's Pops's old friend. I'll check out this Antony for you."

Her chest tightened as if Cupid reached past her rib cage and squeezed her heart with his pudgy hand. Part of her loved that Oli was willing to help her. Another part wanted him to rant, to come between her and Antony like he'd done with Ronnie Landon. Come to think of it, Oli *had* acted jealous. No, that was a silly thought. He'd been an overprotective brother she hadn't needed. So why did the idea of him throwing a fit of jealousy make a deliciously wicked warmth bloom in her chest?

"How about I treat you to breakfast in town?"

He grinned. "Want to show me off?"

She laughed. "Well, it's not often you come home. I might have to wait another decade for this opportunity."

"I doubt that." He drained his mug, placed the cup on the tray, then captured her cheek. "Mm, bacon, eggs, waffles? You have yourself a date, Ms. Blue." He shucked her on her chin, then sauntered out of the study. "Let me hop in the shower first."

She released a breath in a whoosh and touched her face, wondering how he managed to spark tingles across her skin. Maybe it was chemistry? Could she be allergic to him? Chuckling at her nonsense, she saved the document and shut down her laptop. A quick shower was a good idea to wash away the silliness and the persistent desire pooling heat in her core. And a stern talking to was exactly what she needed. Act normal? Sure, but something told her she was doomed to fail.

Chapter Six

WHO THE FUCK WAS Antony? Oliver was so furious; he almost tore off the yoga pants. "Well, things just got complicated." He glared at himself in the bathroom mirror. He didn't need a damn shower, but a cold one would be wise after the night he'd had.

He shouldn't have kissed Navy.

Rubbing a hand over his face, he took turns cursing and smiling. She'd kissed him back, hence the victorious grin and the sparkle in his eyes. Her unexpected response had rattled his control. He'd been forced to retreat.

Still, it had shown promise that she could see him in a romantic light.

He chuckled. Not to mention her antics to escape him. Pretending to sleep without smiling had been an effort. The TV's reflection showed her crawling around the island into the kitchen then peeking over the counter. He'd drifted off to her typing, the sound of which recalled their erotic phone calls.

Her alarm had woken him, but when it hadn't interrupted her, he made coffee, needing to discover if his impetuous kiss had affected their friendship.

Well, it hadn't, except for her continuous blushes and her admiring glances. Keeping his cock soft when her gasps and pebbled nipples thwarted his efforts... Well, he deserved a medal, that's for damn sure.

So, he had a right to be happy, but not with another man in the picture. "Maybe Antony's shy?" *Had he honestly said that?* He arched a brow at his reflection. "What the hell were you thinking, Oliver Trent?" He rubbed his chest, rested his hand on his sternum, then stroked his skin with his thumb. He'd find out soon enough what he was up against.

Leaving the bathroom, he yanked underwear on, jeans, a long-sleeved T-shirt in blue-gray, and heavy hiking boots. Almost brand new, they pinched his feet despite the thickest socks he could find. After splashing on cologne, he ran his fingers through his hair until it stood up like he'd just slid out of bed.

"Go get her, Trent." He nodded at the mirror then left his room, striding down the hallway to the kitchen. And paused.

Navy wore skinny jeans that hugged her legs to her ass, and a tight white T-shirt rippled when her breasts bounced. A song played on her phone, and she danced around the kitchen while she cleaned.

Fuck. He almost spun on his heels to take that cold shower he'd skipped.

"Ready?" She flicked out the damp cloth, draped it over the sink, then dried her hands on the kitchen towel. Switching off her phone, she shoved it into her back pocket and rushed past him to the coat hooks. He caught a tantalizing whiff of her floral perfume. "Are you all right?" She arched a brow while she slipped into her jacket, jiggled her breasts again, and exposed a sliver of skin between her T-shirt and jeans.

"Yeah," he croaked. "Just happy to be home."

She grinned. "Not as ecstatic as I am. Holy sugar, Oli, I *have* missed you."

A wave of intense emotion engulfed his chest, and he swooped, scooping her into his arms for a crushing hug. He buried his nose in the curve of her neck, granted the opportunity to inhale her perfume without judgment.

"Ditto, Blue." He cleared his throat and released her, not needing a hard-on just as their day began. Still, he slid her down his body, letting her feel every inch of him. "Forgiven me yet for Ronnie?"

She winced. "I get why you went into big-brother mode, but you embarrassed me at my party *and* told me I looked like a slut."

He pinched his lips and studied the pain darkening her blue eyes. Big-brother mode? So, she hadn't thought he'd been jealous? "I'm sorry. I was just so angry with Gray who didn't give a shit that night, forcing me to protect you. Ronnie wasn't and still isn't good enough for you, Blue. He was a dick, and you know it."

"He was the most handsome man in town. Now look, he has a wife, kids, and I have…" She gestured with a sweep of her hand. "Nada, nothing."

"He wouldn't have married you, Navy. You'd have been a fuck and a notch on his endless bedpost."

She winced. "You can't know that."

"I can. Boys talk in the locker room. Everyone there wanted to fuck you. Mind you, they never said so in the vicinity of Gray. He'd have killed them."

Her eyes widened then narrowed. "But—"

"Ronnie had a bet going that he'd fuck you on your pink bed on your birthday." Oliver cupped her face, holding her still. "I didn't know how to tell you or whether you'd believe me."

She gaped, the deep pink of her mouth tempting him more than he cared to admit. "That's so cliché."

He grinned. "I know, right?" Drawing her into his arms, he rested his chin on the crown of her head and ran his hand up and down her back. "I thought for sure you'd kick him to the curb. But when you two disappeared into your room..."

She slumped and hugged him. "So, I'm alone forever?" She raised her gaze to his.

"You'll always have me, Blue." He kissed her temple.

She snorted. "You'll marry, have kids, move away. I'll be that old woman baking gingerbread for children not her own. My womb will dry up and turn to dust, Oli." She leaned back to run a fingertip along the bridge of his nose. "I'm *so* sorry I broke your nose."

He laughed, happy to have glossed over his true motivations. "I was furious *and* impressed."

"Then I made it worse by ignoring you." She slipped her arms around his neck for a quick hug, pressing her breasts against his chest. "Please forgive me, Oli." She jerked away. "Wait. You *should* have told me, regardless of how I might've reacted."

"Agreed." He captured her hand for a kiss, then twirled her on the spot.

Chuckling, she unhooked his jacket mid-twirl and offered it to him. "You're just lucky I love you."

Fire exploded in his chest in a bright burst of joy. He stilled, the jacket halfway on. Then reality doused the flames in ice. She loved him as a brother.

The drive into town was made in silence. No tension thickened the air, demanding he cut it with pointless words. Colefield had changed, as expected after a decade. If he judged the well-maintained curbs and roads, it was flourishing too. Bold and bright signage above clean glass shopfronts, the bustling sidewalks teemed with families greeting each other or stopping to chat. Picturesque in white snow and colorful decorations, it was clear why Navy hadn't left.

"Stop by the fire station first. Let me meet this Antony."

She glanced at him but said nothing, just parked in a bay outside the brick building. "Want me to come in?"

"Yup," he grinned. After climbing out, he waited for her, offering her his hand.

She took it without hesitation and let him lead her. "This isn't necessary, Oli. I'm not that invested."

"If you don't find out once and for all, it will haunt you." He stepped into the bay, tugging her with him. Her cheeks bloomed, proving Antony mattered. "Hello?"

A man popped his head out from behind a fire truck.

"Hey." Oliver waved. "Is Chief Henderson in?"

"That's Max to you." A large man barreled toward him, a grin splitting his cheeks. Oliver dropped Blue's hand and accepted the hug, wincing at the hearty thumps to his back. "Why didn't you tell me you were coming?"

"Surprise?" Oliver grinned.

"Sure is." Max laughed then faced Blue. "Thanks for bringing him, Navy. I have to tell you, Oliver, she's a gem. Every week a batch of cupcakes arrive, and oh my soul, are they divine." Max rubbed his washboard stomach. "I have to put in extra time at the gym, but so worth it."

Blue beamed. "Glad you like them, Chief."

"Like them?" Max scoffed. "Harry said he had to ask you not to do it for the precinct. Said his men were getting too fat."

Her ears glowed. Oliver took pity on her and looped his arm around her, pulling her into the curve of his body. She didn't resist but rested her hand on his stomach, like they hugged all the time.

"Just thought we'd pop in on our way to breakfast," Oliver said, excusing the visit.

"Appreciate it, Oliver. How's Eddie?"

Oliver chuckled. "Pops's itching to return to Colefield. Sure, the temperate clime doesn't irritate his joints, but he was never one for the beach."

"Will he?" Blue peered at Oliver. "Come home, that is?"

He nodded. "He's just finalizing a few things before he arrives."

She squealed and left Oliver's arms to do the Charleston. He chuckled, reveling in her antics. Holy shit, joy saturated every part of her. Her gaze snagged on someone, and whoever it was, eradicated her excitement. She swallowed and returned to Oliver's side as if she sought shelter. He glanced behind him and did a slow nod at the dark-haired man carrying a hose reel.

Antony.

The man was tallish, a little on the lanky side, but attractive. And just like that, Oliver had a plan.

"I'm staying at Blue's. Call if you want to go for a beer, Max." He kissed her temple, lingering longer than was necessary. "Ready for breakfast, sweetheart?"

She waved at Max. "See you next week."

"Thanks for stopping by." Max shoved his hands into his fire dex pants and watched them leave.

"Oli, what the hell was that?" Blue whispered as soon as she reached her SUV.

"I'll explain over breakfast." He wanted to rub his palms together and cackle.

Antony wasn't a threat. The man hadn't even glanced at Blue. So the plan the fire station visit had inspired was foolproof.

Five minutes later, she parked outside Milly's, climbed out and slammed the SUV's door.

"Trust me, Blue." He caught her wrist and stalled her. "Please."

She sighed, and her shoulders sagged. "Fine." She chose a table by the window, suiting him.

As soon as he sat, he snagged her hand and ran his thumb across her knuckles. "Let's order. Then I'll let you in on my brilliant idea."

A smile twitched her lips. "How did I stay angry with you for so long?"

"You were a force to be reckoned with as a teenager."

"What?" she squeaked. "What am I now?"

"The most beautiful woman in Colefield." He flashed his broadest grin.

She laughed. "There's like fifty eligible women in this town, Oli."

"I'm entitled to my opinion." He winked.

"Charmer." She tugged her hand free to peruse the menu.

A waitress with graying blonde hair smiled, her pen ready. "What'll you have, Navy?"

"A cappuccino with whipped cream and the Morning Sunrise, Milly. Eggs over easy, bacon crispy."

"Make that two." He snatched the menu out of Blue's hand and handed it to the waitress. "Oh, and a stack of waffles, please."

When they were alone, he clasped her hand again. "Right. Here's my strategy to win you Antony. What if we make him jealous?"

Her eyes widened, and for a moment, as he drowned in their blue depths, his thoughts scattered. "What do you mean make him jealous? Oli, that implies he cares."

"Oh, he cares. He'd be a fool not to, Blue." No guilt assaulted Oliver for that outright lie. All's fair in love, right?

She snorted. "And how do you propose to make him jealous? Wait. Do I get a makeover?" She bounced on her seat, jiggling her breasts.

"Why?" He squeezed her hand, wishing he could touch other parts of her. Shit, he was an idiot to love the one woman he shouldn't. But there was no stopping this, not when his heart was hers. "You're perfect as you are."

"Right." She leaned forward, resting her elbows on the table. "And how do you plan to perform this miracle?"

"I will woo you; dinner, dancing, midnight picnics—"

"Picnics? It's freezing." She glanced out the window at the light snowfall.

"Exactly." He wiggled his eyebrows. "Any man in love with you wouldn't want you snuggling with someone else."

"Are you sure this is going to work?" She nibbled on her lip like he longed to do. "I mean...what if he doesn't notice?"

"Then you'll know where you stand *and* would've spent time with me."

She grinned. "The latter is definitely a plus."

His heart skipped a beat, spreading a flutter through his chest. "Same. So, are you in?"

She narrowed her eyes. "Mm, what's the catch?"

He sucked a deep breath in, preparing to risk it all. "You have to pretend to be falling in love with me."

She frowned. "Isn't that a little extreme?"

"I'm deeply offended." He harumphed for effect. "Am I not lovable?"

She chuckled. "You are the most lovable man in Colefield."

"Touché." He rolled his bottom lip under the top. "Truth is, Blue, guys want what other guys have."

She ran her gaze over him, her cheeks blooming a beautiful peach. "What would I need to do?"

"Cuddle, hug, hold hands...maybe a kiss if the opportunity presents itself."

"Kiss?" she squeaked. "Holy sh...sugar, Oli, you'd kiss me?"

His heart did the Tango. *Fuck yeah*, he wanted to roar. "Yup." He dragged out the word. "Whatever it takes."

She smiled—the one he loved—broad, bright, filled with untamed joy. But tears shimmered in her eyes. "How'd I get so lucky having you as my oldest friend?"

"Blame Gray, it's easier." Oliver kissed her knuckles and leaned back, releasing her for the cappuccinos Milly slid onto the table.

"When and how do we start?" Blue scooped cream off the top of her coffee and popped the dollop into her mouth. He blinked, willing himself not to stare at the way her lips crinkled and the soft sucking noises she made.

"I was thinking a public kiss. Get the tongues wagging." He poured sugar into his coffee, sneaking peeks at her, praying she was done torturing him with her mouth. "Nothing hurts a man more than hearing via the grapevine his crush has a suitor."

"Despite how logical this all sounds, it's insane, Oli." She shook her head, tossing her curls wild. "I mean, we haven't established whether the man likes me."

"Well, let's see what happens if he doesn't and we did all this for nothing." He ticked off on his fingers. "You have dinner *with me*. You go dancing *with me*. You have a midnight picnic *with me*. Sure, a few kisses might be an inconvenience, but hey, after a decade apart, I don't mind." He smothered the wince at his understatement. "I want to catch up on wasted years, Blue. Get to know the amazing woman you've become."

"Fine. As long as you promise you won't do anything that makes you...uncomfortable."

He almost snorted at that. As he sat there, he was semi-hard and straining his jeans. Did that count as uncomfortable? "Deal." He smirked. "Want to have a safe word?"

She laughed again. "Sure. Pomegranate."

He arched a brow at her quick response. "And you have to work that into the conversation."

"Oh." She gasped. "Challenge accepted, Oliver Dylan Trent."

"We shall see, Navy Anna Sanders." He sliced a piece of bacon and popped it into his mouth, grinning at her while he chewed.

Chapter Seven

THIS WAS INSANE. NOT that Navy minded holding Oli's hand, but damn, every time he touched her, something bubbled inside her, like molten lava with a one-way path to her...sex. Heat spread across her cheeks, burning her skin despite the crisp air. She glanced at her thigh where his hand rested. Getting into character, he'd called it.

Still, the comfortable yet exhilarating weight of his hand snagged her focus. She struggled to keep her gaze on the road. When his fingers twitched, fresh tingles rippled up her leg and hitched her breath. She was a fool to agree to his silly plan.

Why had she? To be wooed, that's why. Dinner, dancing, and a picnic sounded divine. She could pretend they were dating. Allow herself this time with Oli, enjoy the attention he'd lavish on her before he left for his city life. She winced. This was a holiday fake-romance, nothing more.

After he abandoned her, she'd return to pining for Antony. She sighed. When the weather turned warm and the church held a picnic, she'd sip her iced tea and ogle Antony's ass in his tight jeans. Maybe she wanted him to stay afar. Maybe, despite the aching loneliness, she didn't want something meaningful with him.

She nibbled her lip as she poked her psyche with a mental finger.

"What has you lost in thought, Blue?"

She peeked at Oli and forced a smile. Telling him she could take or leave Antony when Oliver had thought of this plan, offered to help her, wanted to wine and dine her? No, she couldn't reveal any of this. She'd have to act delighted *if* Antony responded to this madness.

"Just running through what I'll need to make Shepherd's Pie. Thankfully, I texted Ray I'd be by to pick up the ground elk instead of him delivering it. Might as well grab a few other things. Got to feed your big ass." Her heart faltered when she scanned him dominating that side of the SUV with his broad shoulders and long legs. He squeezed her thigh and drew a squeak from her. "How long are you staying?"

"Undecided."

"What? You can do that?" She glanced at him while parking the SUV in front of the butchery. Did that mean he'd be with her for longer than a few days? Excitement made her giddy, and she swallowed a giggle.

"It's my business, so yes, the boss can be away for as long as he wants." Oli held out his hand as soon as they'd exited the car.

She took it, relishing the warmth of his fingers laced through hers. Without gloves, they should be cold, but the skin-on-skin sent a spark of heat through her. Wow, she should bottle that and sell it to the lonely women in Colefield.

She twitched, realizing he was waiting for her to respond. "Oh? Well, I wish I could do the same. I use my weekends to catch up on orders."

"Morning, Navy. Is that you, Trent?" Ray circled the counter while wiping his hands before he held one out to Oli. "It's good to see you."

Oli accepted it for a shake. "Hello, Ray. I'm glad to be here." Oli tugged Navy into his arms and gazed at her upturned face. "And Pops's coming soon."

"Wonderful. Eddie's hunting skills are legendary." Ray returned behind the counter, folding chunks of meat into wax paper.

Navy tapped the glass display, choosing what she wanted. One by one, the meat joined a pile that Ray would ring up for her. After each selection, Oli drew her back to his side.

Ray wiped his hand on a cloth hanging from his apron's sash. "I'm hoping the new owner of the lodge will be as obliging with their kills. Any idea who he is? Do you think he'd be open to doing business?"

"He will be." Oli grinned and offered his hand for another shake. "We'll iron out the details later."

She froze, gaping at him. Ray beamed like a prize fisherman. Anger bubbled up, blinding her. She punched Oli on the chest. "When the hell were you going to tell me?" Her breathing shuddered at what this meant. A tear slipped past her defenses. "You're moving back?"

He nodded while rubbing his chest. "Permanently."

She squealed. Joy exploded like a thousand sparklers. Throwing her arms around him, she crushed him in a hug. She buried her face in the curve of his neck and let the tears flow. He embraced her, running his hand up her back, and held her close.

"All good then." Ray held out her parcel. She had to pull away to accept pay for it. "And Gray?"

At this question, she waited for Oli to answer, her heart thumping in her ears.

He brushed curls off her face and, with his thumb, wiped away her tears. His hazel eyes swirled with intense emotion she couldn't name. "Gray will be in and out. It's a joint venture."

She beamed and hugged him again, relishing every one of his defined ridges, but something niggled her mind. "So, you bought the lodge? Are you making it a *hunting* lodge?" She sliced her attention between Oli and a grinning Ray.

"Yup." Oli smiled, excited about this new venture, no doubt. "We plan to bring tourism to Colefield."

Ice slithered from her ears to her toes. "By killing elk?"

"Moose, reindeer, bison, bears..."

She squeaked, waved at Ray, and stomped out. Oli caught up to her on the sidewalk, directing families around them.

"I can't believe it. Why would you do this? There are people needing the meat to survive, Oli. You know that." She tried to go around him, but he thwarted her, forcing her to stand still or hit him again.

"Do you want to hear our plans or are you going to throw a tantrum right here?" He smiled at a passing mother ushering two toddlers along.

Navy's vision edged with red. Fury consumed her again, on par with the Ronnie-incident. "Tantrum?" She swung a fist, prepared to break Oliver's nose again.

He caught her punch and yanked her across the divide between them. With his arm looped around her, pinning her fist behind her, he held her against him. She tried to wiggle out of his embrace. He squeezed, limiting the space she had to break free. Cupping her cheek, he forced her to meet his gaze.

She glared, hating that he was stronger than her, despite the inner damsel squealing at his dominance. "Let. Me. Go."

"It hurts, Blue, that you think I'd harm this community." He stroked her chin. "That Gray would, renowned wildlife photographer that he is."

Her breath caught. Pain darkened Oli's hazel eyes. Guilt panged across her heart. She *had* thought the worst of him and shouldn't have. He was right to point that out. "So, you're not going to hunt for sport?"

"Of course we are."

She kicked him on the shin, firing bolts of agony along her toes through her boot. With a yelp, he thrust her away but caught her wrist, spinning her into his arms. The second he slashed his mouth across hers, she stilled, her breath freezing in her lungs. The public kiss. Now? She shrieked, wiggling to free herself. He tightened his hold, with one hand clasping her neck, his thumb under her jaw to keep her in place.

She opened her mouth to lambaste him, but he slipped his tongue between her lips. Her senses exploded like this morning's kiss, and all that pent-up lust slammed into her. She whimpered, succumbing to his tongue mastery, letting him lead. Anger merged into a blaze of need, and she dropped the parcel to cling to him, tilting her head for easier access. He groaned and deepened the kiss, setting her blood on fire. His scent filled her nose, and the solid muscle under her fingers urged her to stroke every inch of him. Something dark, addictive, and hot uncoiled in her core.

His tentative foray on the couch couldn't compare to whatever this was.

Holy sugar. She needed to up the chemistry in her novels. They were a timid representation of the inferno engulfing her.

He released her, his breathing ragged. His gaze snagged hers, his eyes burning with need. At least, she recognized that emotion. When she struck his cheek, he gaped. He wasn't as stunned as she was at her audacity. That ever-present guilt twanged at the sight of a red palm print forming.

She spun on a heel, scooped up the parcel of meat, and marched to the SUV, sliding in without a glance at the gathered crowds. The passenger door opened, and Oli climbed in, slamming the door.

"The slap was a bit much," he rasped, rubbing his cheek.

She blinked at him, fury still tainting her vision. "Slap? Kiss? Buying the lodge? Can't quite decide, Oli." She started the engine and reversed, not wanting to say another word to him.

The last day had been amazing having him home, but now, she wanted him out of her house and her life. He had nowhere to go, not with the Shoot and Toot in town. She was stuck with him.

"Do you want to hear our plan or not?" His whispered words sliced through her furious thoughts.

She glared. "You're killing for sport. No matter how you phrase it, that fact doesn't change."

"All kills *during* hunting season will be donated to the community."

She gaped at him. "Your clients won't be taking the meat home?"

"Nope, it's part of the program. When not hunting, we'll be raising, restocking, and rehabilitating."

Her anger fizzled as swiftly as it had formed. "Truly?"

"Yup. We have Nat. Geo's backing, Blue." Oli faced forward but rested his hand on her thigh. "It's why Pops's coming back. He'll manage the hunting side of the lodge. I'll do the financials and marketing. Gray's the celebrity, photographing and filming the events we plan to host. There'll be a spa, bird watching, and stargazing. For the kids, we'll have snow machine races, snowball fights, and a petting zoo."

It was a brilliant business idea, bringing tourists to Colefield as well as creating jobs. "Sounds good," she croaked, tears burning behind her eyes at the way she'd overreacted.

He squeezed her thigh. "I love how passionate you are about your community and environment, Blue. But it worries me that you don't trust me." He released her leg to tuck curls behind her ear. She shivered at his delicate touch. "I get it. We've been apart for a decade. You don't know me anymore."

He was right, but his softly spoken words didn't ease the burn of shame. She *should* have trusted him. They had a history. And in her past dealings with him, he'd proven trustworthy.

"You're right." She let the tears slip free. Driving was safer with her hands on the wheel, not wiping her damp cheeks, despite the urge to do so. 'I'm sorry."

As soon as she pulled into the garage and switched off the engine, she twisted in her seat to face him. "I..." She hesitated, not knowing what to say.

He cupped her cheek and wiped it with the pad of his thumb. "At least we'll get to know each other over the next few days."

She nodded, nuzzling his palm.

His breath caught, and the tension in the cab thickened. He leaned across and captured her lips with his. When she grasped his jacket to keep him near, he deepened the kiss, stealing her senses again.

He jerked back to rub a hand over his face. "I shouldn't have kissed you, Blue. Now I want to all the time."

"I see that." She smiled through the desire scratching at her control. "Come, the pie won't make itself, and I do believe I promised you a homecoming meal."

He climbed out of the SUV and plugged it into the wall socket. "It *is* almost lunchtime."

She removed her jacket and hung it on a hook. "Fine, I'll make you a three-cheese grilled sandwich. That should tide you over." She strode into the kitchen, packed the meat into the freezer, and placed the wrapped ground elk on the counter.

He slid onto the barstool and watched her, with his elbows on the counter and his chin on a raised palm.

"I said I wouldn't ask, but when's Gray coming?"

He shrugged. "He's in Africa. Despite planning his itinerary, I have learned to leave the return journey in his hands. I went with him once." He winced. "We were in the same spot for days, waiting for the right time, situation, lighting to capture the perfect photo. His patience is extraordinary. Outside of that, he's a bear, growling and grumpy. Also, he can sleep anywhere. For a week, mosquitoes feasted on me. I couldn't catch a wink."

"That's what you do? Book his trips?"

"It's how our business started. We expanded into an agency that designs and organizes any trip anywhere in the world. We developed so many contacts, that if you want to experience something, we'll source it."

"And you're running your company from the lodge?" She frowned. "Or are you selling?"

"Businesses can be managed from anywhere these days. We'll keep the staff we have but most have the option to work from home."

She buttered slices of ciabatta, layered cheddar, Emmenthal, gouda, sprinkled salt and cayenne pepper, and closed it. Another smear of butter on the top, and she flipped it, resting it on the hot skillet. "Do you have to return to Anham to pack?"

"Done and dusted. Expecting the truck any day now."

She froze with the butter knife in her hand. "But, Oli, where will you be staying? Is the lodge livable?" A smear of butter on the topside preceded a spatula flip.

"I'm staying with you, Blue. My stuff will go into storage until I'm ready. All has been organized."

She grinned. "Sorry. Forgot who I was talking to."

He studied her in silence. "Would you say we've had our first argument...as a couple?"

She snapped her gaze to his. "Sure."

"And now for make-up sex?" His hazel eyes twinkled.

Even though he wasn't serious, her mind went there. What if he circled the island, slipped the spatula out of her hand, and kissed her? Heat burst across her face, and she inched closer to the pan, hoping he thought the steam rising was the reason for her flushed cheeks.

"Sex? What's that?" she joked. Grabbing a plate, she placed his grilled ciabatta onto it and pushed it across to him. "Soda? Coffee? Tea? Water? Fruit juice?"

"A soda, please. I'd better pick up beers." He bit into his grilled sandwich and moaned. "So good."

A knock intruded as she placed her buttered ciabatta onto the skillet. "It's open!"

Sheriff Harry Martin strolled in, slapping his wide-brimmed hat on his khaki-covered thigh. "Hi, Navy... Heard Oliver was in town and assumed said vehicle stuck in the ditch was his."

"Come on in, bestie." She beamed at Harry. "Want a grilled sandwich?"

"If you're making?" Harry chose a barstool and shook Oli's pinkie, the only clean part of his hands. "Welcome back. Mayor Kelley will be delighted you arrived safely."

While she prepped another sandwich, she listened as the two men discussed towing Oli's vehicle to the repair shop. When she placed the grilled sandwich on a plate and slid it across to Harry, she winked. "I won't mention this to Beth."

His wife had him on a low-carb diet this season. Last year, he'd lived on nothing but watermelon. That was the real reason he wouldn't allow cupcakes in the precinct.

Before he devoured the sandwich, he rubbed his gray beard, his eyes sparkling. "See that you keep this a secret, Ms. Sanders."

She laughed and flipped her sandwich. "How did we do in the Shoot and Toot?"

"Came second. Not too bad considering Renford has a new deputy. The woman hit every mark. She's an ex-military sniper." He grinned. "Now the Toot part starts."

The festival meant the center of town would be insanely busy because the tourism brought in so much revenue. Next year, they'd hold it at a neighboring town to boost their economy.

"She must be impressive." Navy tilted her head. A woman sniper would make an excellent main character. Navy dismissed the thought. The learning curve would be too steep when she knew nothing about guns.

"Hell yeah, blonde, petite, but she can heft a Barrett M82. That's almost thirty pounds to you uninitiated." Harry winked.

Gathering a few sodas, bottles of water, and a jug of fruit juice, Navy positioned them in front of the men. With her grilled ciabatta in hand, she waved at Harry. "Let me grant you two a little privacy. I'll be in my office if you need me." With a soda, she bolted down the hall and into her study. She pressed her back against the door and sighed, grateful for the time alone.

While she ate her meal, she booted up her laptop, eager to punch more sexual tension into the 'pin against the wall' scene. Afterward, she'd run it by Oli, just in case. No point in offending her biggest fan. She smiled, licked her fingers, wiped her hands on a paper napkin, and tried to capture a little of what Oli made her feel.

Chapter Eight

Oliver wasn't furious. No, he was beyond that. He flicked a glance across the seat at Tammy, his ex-girlfriend from high school. The passing years had been more than kind to her. Long blonde hair cascaded around her, bright green eyes glimmered with that youthful mischief that had once captivated him. But it wasn't Tammy who tormented his nights.

Sure, he'd left with Harry to avoid taking Navy on her kitchen counter. Distance to bolster his control seemed the best approach. The town had welcomed him like the prodigal son, and the talk with the mayor solidified his intentions toward the hunting lodge and its future.

But when Navy hadn't answered his calls... He gritted his teeth. Harry had gone home for the night, stranding Oliver. Which meant catching a taxi. When Tammy had offered to drop him off, rejecting it would've been rude. Still, when she stroked his thigh then squeezed his knee, he'd captured her hand and set it aside.

He clenched his fingers until his knuckles were white, keeping his fist on his thigh to prevent another caress. Why the fuck hadn't Navy answered? Why hadn't he thought to use her vehicle?

With a mumbled thanks, he bolted out of the truck as soon as Tammy stopped at the bottom of Navy's driveway. Not glancing back, he strode-jogged toward the front door, but the slam of a truck door made him wince.

He entered the house. Fifties music played in the background. The dining table was set, dead candles and unused wine glasses sliced through his anger. One place was missing its plate. The aroma of Elk Shepherd's Pie pressed on his heart and stung his eyes with unshed tears. For a moment, he expected his mom to waltz in. He half-turned to the passage that remained empty.

"Where's Navy?" Tammy paused too close to him—her rose perfume made his nose itch.

He was the first to admit he'd broken her heart, ending their relationship a week before prom and the day after Navy's sixteenth birthday party. It hadn't felt right dating one woman when he loved another.

"Hang on, let me fetch her." He strode down the passage, desperate to pull away from Tammy. The drive here had been awkward. He'd moved on, but Tammy still lived in the past.

Before Navy's office, he paused, staring at her closed bedroom door. She'd better be asleep, sick as a dog, elbows deep in writing...or else. He tapped on the office door and peeked in. "Blue?"

With her back to the door, her shoulders twitched, then drooped as if she was sad. He tightened his grip on the door until the wood creaked.

"I...waited for you." She spun her chair to face him. Her eyes were red and puffy. Had she been crying?

"I called you four times." No way would he feel guilty despite the familiar twinges wrenching his gut.

Her eyes widened. "What?" She leapt out of her chair and hurried to her room.

He followed her, finding her rifling through her jeans.

"Oh." She flicked her thumb across her phone's screen. "I'm sorry, Oli. Here I thought you were being an ass." She grinned. "Why did you call?"

He sighed. "I needed a ride."

"Hello?" Tammy's voice traveled along the passage.

Blue stilled and crowded him. "Who's that?" she whispered, resting her hand on his forearm.

"My ride." He grimaced.

She gasped, her lips forming a perfect 'oh.' Veering around him, she missed the hand he'd raised to stroke her cheek.

"Navy?" Tammy stepped into view at the end of the passage.

"Hi, Tammy!" Blue's welcome was too boisterous. "Thanks for bringing Oli *home*. I'm sorry I missed his calls." She arched a brow at Oli while he struggled to hide a grin. Was she jealous? "Next time, take my car." Her look implied he was a dumbass. After the last fifteen minutes with Tammy, he couldn't agree more.

Blue slipped around Tammy to grab a jacket and tug it on. "Let me walk you to your car."

"Okay." Tammy settled a hopeful smile on him. "Looking forward to seeing you around town, Oliver." She ran a gaze over him, lingering on parts of him covered by his coat.

"Sure," he said, not wanting to delay her departure.

Blue left the front door open while she ushered Tammy down the driveway. He waved from the doorway when Tammy glanced over her shoulder. The moment her focus shifted, he threw himself behind the wooden fence running the length of the driveway. Scrambling across the snow, he trailed them. The front of him chilled while he leopard crawled.

"Uh, Navy, you and Oliver have been friends for ages." Tammy cleared her throat. "Do you know if he's seeing anyone?"

His breath hitched. He held while he waited for Blue's response.

"In the city? No, he was not."

Shit. Air rushed out of his lungs. That opened the door to Tammy's advances. He thumped the snow, sending up mini clouds of flakes.

"His heart's broken, Tammy." Navy paused. "I'm sorry."

Great. Sure, that lie made him unavailable to Tammy, but it also put Blue out of the running.

"Oh, no. I'm sad to hear that." A car door opened. "I was hoping to rekindle our...friendship."

"Oli's not the same as when we were kids, Tammy. Even I'm relearning who he's become. But you can try. No law against that."

He scowled. Nope. The ride over and the lack of sparks between them confirmed his instincts. He blew on his cupped hands, trying to warm them.

"Is he planning on getting his own place, Navy?"

"I don't know, but Oli's welcome to stay with me forever."

He grinned. *Yes, think along those lines, sweetheart. Forever with my ring on your finger.*

"Rumor has it, you two are dating." At Tammy's question, he wanted to peer over the top of the fence. Seeing Blue's face when she responded was almost too tempting to risk a peek.

"Yes, we're dating." Her voice rasped across his senses. Despite it being a lie to her, it was the truth for him. They *were* dating, and if he had his way, she'd believe it too.

"I was hoping you'd step aside, y'know, because of our history." Tammy was being her old persistent self.

Blue laughed. "Oli's an opinionated man who goes after what he wants. If he wanted to date you, I wouldn't be able to dissuade him."

He smothered a chuckle. *Well said.*

"And besides, even if we don't work out, do you want him on the rebound?"

He couldn't resist using the fence to clamber to his knees to sneak a peek. The streetlamps illuminated Tammy's pursed lips as she slid into the car.

"Night, Navy."

Shit. He ducked and scrambled for the house, slipping inside to sprint to his room for a quick shower. Despite needing to thaw, he rushed through his ablutions before donning his yoga pants and T-shirt.

Blue was in the kitchen, warming a serving of pie if he judged the revived aroma correctly. She gestured to the dining table.

He shook his head. The abandoned setting served as a reminder of the epic failure this night had been. "The couch will do." Taking the plate from her, he sank into the right side of the double seater. She took the other end.

He snuck glances at her while he dug his fork through the mashed potatoes to the ground elk beneath. The aroma tantalized him when he raised the loaded fork to his mouth. At the first bite, he moaned, savoring the explosion of flavors across his tongue.

"You used sherry?"

She nodded.

Tears burned the backs of his eyes. *Just like Mom's.* The sweetness of sherry instead of red wine, added to the wildness of the elk. He treasured every bite. Every mouthful heightened his love for Blue, who embodied his past and, he hoped, his future.

"Good?" She smiled and rested her cheek on the back of the couch, watching him eat.

"Better than I remember."

"So, the next time you want to eavesdrop, make sure I don't see you." She laughed. "Dumbass."

He almost choked on the next bite. His cheeks burned when he coughed.

"You're just lucky the fresh snow softened the ground."

She was right. He'd have crunched had the snow been harder. "Sorry, Blue. She hit on me in the car."

"Oh?" Navy's brow shot up. "What did she say?"

"Nothing." He shrugged. How to convey how he'd felt, how guilt had twisted his insides? In his mind and heart, he belonged to Blue. Silly, right? Like all women would know that? "She rubbed my thigh. I damn near hugged the door after that." He'd been too furious to offer his usual gentle rejection. Bad planning on his part had put him in that situation. He only had himself to blame.

Blue frowned. "But you touch my leg. I struggle to see the problem."

He placed the empty plate onto the coffee table, captured her hand, and tugged her closer. Placing her hand on his thigh, he trapped it under his.

With Tammy, he'd felt nothing, like draping a cloth napkin across his lap. With Blue, her touch burned him through his pants, sending electricity to his groin in swift, sharp bolts of intense pleasure.

In a slow demonstration, he dragged her hand from his knee to an inch from his hardening cock. He watched her face, mesmerized by her parted lips and the blue swirling in her eyes.

"Like that." He cleared his throat, but hoarseness clung to his voice. "I felt...violated."

She snatched her hand away. "I'm...sorry. I had no idea."

He recaptured her hand and rested it on his thigh again. "I don't feel that way with you."

She blinked.

He studied her expressive face, wondering if she'd pick up on the implication—that he wanted to fuck her hard, all night and into the day. "I'm not attracted to Tammy."

"Makes sense. If a man I didn't like touched me like this, my skin would crawl."

Nope. Oliver grinned. She missed the hint completely. He squeezed her knee through her leggings and slid his fingers up to mid-thigh. "Does this repulse you?"

She shook her head. Her cheeks bloomed, and she licked her bottom lip. "Dessert?" She leapt off the couch, trailing his fingers across her thigh.

"Sure." If she meant herself.

She danced back to him, carrying two small plates.

He blinked at the large slice of lemon meringue she offered him. "You didn't." Trying to convey how much she meant to him, he met and held her gaze.

"There's a whole pie." Her slice was a third the size of his.

When she handed him a cake fork, he made sure to brush her fingers with his. Her eyelashes fluttered. Her lips twitched before she broke the connection. After she settled on her end of the couch, he dipped his gaze to the dessert—a pie he hadn't eaten since his mom last made it.

"How...did you remember this is my favorite?" He dug his fork in, shoving a large bite into his mouth. *Holy fuck.* Blue would be the death of him. This much deliciousness in one evening? The sweetness clenched his cheeks, but the lemony tang swept across his senses. He groaned, shoveling in another mouthful. While he chewed, he peeked at her. A bite lodged in his throat when she licked her cake fork.

"Don't do that," he rasped.

Her eyes widened as she flicked her flattened tongue across the back of the fork. "Do what?" Smacking her lips, she stacked the plates and placed the fork on the top.

"Lick your fork."

She blushed. "My table manners aren't citified enough for you?" She folded her legs and rested her chin on her knees.

"You lick the fork like a trained courtesan." He growled the words, uncaring how gravelly his voice had become. "How have you stayed single all these years?"

"If I tell you, I'd have to kill you." She shrugged. "Colefield doesn't have eligible men unless you snagged one in high school." She arched a brow at him. "I could've been Mrs. Ronnie Landon."

"You would've been miserable."

"Maybe, maybe not." She stroked her belly. "I'd have been a mom, though." Wistfulness darkened her eyes as she stared into the dying fire in the hearth.

"You want children?" He did...with her. Images of her dancing around the kitchen with a toddler on her hip skewered him.

"Yes." The smile gracing her lips was wide and filled with love. She adored her future children already. "Don't you?"

"Very much."

"Well, if I hit thirty without finding love, you can donate your sperm to the Knock-Up Navy fund."

"You'll find love soon." Shit, he hoped she returned his affection.

She snorted.

He brushed a curl off her cheek. "Trust me, Blue."

Her eyes narrowed as she studied him. "What do you know that you're not sharing, Oli?" Her frown deepened. She nibbled on her lip while flicking her gaze over him. "About Antony—"

"It's too soon to know." He forced a smile. There was no way he'd let her pull out of his subtle seduction. "Tomorrow's the date, so dress to kill."

She rolled her eyes. "I could slide naked down the fireman's pole, and he wouldn't notice."

Oli hardened to his full length imagining a naked Blue doing anything. He squirmed in his seat, wincing at the burning lust he couldn't extinguish...not yet.

"I'd have to lubricate the pole first." She chuckled. "If Chief would let me."

Oli chuckled, picturing Blue asking Max and the expression the older man would wear. "There goes your writer mind."

She stilled. "You didn't tell Gray?"

He scowled. "You asked me not to."

Her shoulders relaxed as she sighed, "Thank you."

He stroked his thumb across her hand warming his thigh. "Why hide it, Blue? Do you think he'll judge you?"

"Yes...and no. He'll tease me endlessly."

Oliver shrugged. "It's his job as your brother."

Pain trembled her cheeks, and tears shimmered on her eyelashes. "I miss him...missed you. I wish things could be like it was when Dad was alive."

He dragged her onto his lap, cradling her against him. "Oh, Blue." He wished he could kiss her as he longed to do.

When she snuggled closer, he rubbed her back. What he wanted was to confess. Why did this have to be so hard? She loved him...as a brother. He needed more. Nuzzling her hair with his chin, he let her cry. Each sob or sniff tugged at his heartstrings. He didn't need the reminder. She'd always affected him, from the time she'd toddled after them as boys, to when she'd almost kissed Ronnie. Her mini skirt had hugged her curves, exposed her legs, and the way Ronnie had touched her...

Oliver gritted his teeth, fighting the ever-present burn of jealousy and the poignant pang of guilt. He'd told her she'd looked like a whore, crushing what confidence had begun to blossom. His careless words had hurt her and cost him more. He'd lost her that day.

At Mom's funeral, a glimmer of the old Navy had appeared. He'd grasped at it, wanting to rebuild their connection. Not that they could ever get back the time they'd lost.

Then she'd called for sexual guidance. He would've given her a kidney to stay in touch with him. Worse than this was that she had no clue how he felt. In her mind and heart, he'd always be Gray's best friend if he didn't do something to change that. He'd lost her before and survived. Though it wasn't what he wanted, to lose her again, he was willing to risk their friendship.

"Blue?" He captured her chin in his hand and tilted her face.

"No, don't look at me." She jerked away. "I'm a mess."

He scoffed. "Worse than the time you had severe heatstroke and swelled like a red balloon?" He captured her cheeks between his palms, forcing her to meet his gaze. "Or the time you had toilet paper stuck in your panties and unraveled the entire roll before you noticed?"

He chuckled at her groan.

"You and Gray just let me walk through the house like that."

You and Gray... There lay his problem. "My point is, a few tears doesn't change how beautiful you are."

She blinked at him. "Oli?" She licked her bottom lip and tightened her grip on his waist. "Are you...*flirting* with me?"

At last! He laughed. "Yes."

She frowned. "But why? And don't say it's to practice for Antony. I know how to flirt."

"Oh, you do?" He arched a brow. "Well...show me."

She squeaked and tried to break away. He held firm.

"Fine." She squared her shoulders. "Tell me I'm beautiful."

He met her gaze and wiggled his brows. "You're beautiful, Blue."

The sensual smile that formed across her lips caught his breath. "In this?" She brushed her fingers across his stomach, sparking a scorching trail, to pinch her top between forefinger and thumb. "You should see me out of it." As she said that, she arched her back enough to thrust her breasts forward.

"I want to," he rasped. "I dream of it." He released her cheeks to grab her shoulders, to slide his fingers down her arms and rest them on her hips. There, he slipped his thumbs under the hem of her shirt and stroked her heated skin.

"You're right." She laughed. "I don't know how to flirt." Pulling out of his embrace, she climbed off the couch, paused to kiss his forehead, and unwittingly thrust his face into her cleavage. Scooping the plates off the coffee table, she strode past the sink, placed them on the side, and faced him. "Good night, Oli."

What? No, he wasn't ready. He scrambled off the couch and opened his mouth to confess his undying love. The click of her door closing silenced him.

Fuck.

Chapter Nine

NAVY SLUMPED AGAINST HER bedroom door. She'd run like the scaredy cat she was. No way did she want Oli's reasons behind his flirting. It would be some nonsense tied to Antony, and she wanted, just for a few minutes, to believe he charmed her because he desired her.

She pressed her fingers to her lips. The way he'd watched her as he slid her hand up his thigh. Those intense hazel eyes had darkened. For some strange reason, the look he'd bestowed upon her snatched her breath. His flirting rattled her too. She wanted to ask him how he was still single? How hadn't he managed to woo his unrequited love? What exactly had happened there?

She ran a bath, needing to calm her frayed nerves. Her thoughts cycled through Oli's every expression and gesture in the last two days. The water cooled, and still, she hadn't soaped or washed her hair. This was silliness. Never had she thought she was the kind of woman to overanalyze.

She scrubbed her face and hair, spilling water onto the floor in her haste. Clambering out of the bath splashed more water over the side of the tub. She stared at the wet floor, curling her lip at the mess. Deciding to let it air dry, she stomped into her bedroom with the bath towel in hand, giving herself a vigorous once over.

"Get your shit together, Navy." She whipped on a nightshirt and opened her door.

Hot milk might help, and failing that, a shot of brandy or rum. As she passed Oli's gaping door, she paused, peering into the shadows to discern the shapes the blankets formed. Moonlight painted an ethereal glow on his muscled arm thrown over his face.

Sighing, she padded barefoot to the kitchen and the cupboard housing the cooking liquors. Straight from the bottle, she swigged the rum. When it hit her stomach, it exploded with delicious warmth. She took another mouthful, swirling it from cheek to cheek.

Between sips, she muttered, "Drinking? Why? It isn't as if he's hit on you. And if he did, how would you react, you frigid cow?" Swig. "And do you want him to?" Double swig. "Okay, you do, then what? If this goes bad, it's bye-bye Oli." She slammed the bottle down, then winced, slicing a glance at the passage. "But if it goes well, this is Oli, Navy. The man who knows you the best." She took a long pull of the rum, capped the bottle and put it into the cupboard. "And he's so sexy."

"Blue? Is that you?" His gruff voice reached her from his bedroom.

She squeaked. Had he heard her? Holy sugar, she had to stop talking to herself.

Leveling an unblinking stare at the passage, she half-expected to see his shadow appear. "Who else could it be?"

Then he was striding toward her, bare-chested, his yoga pants hanging low on his hips, exposing his Adonis belt. She swallowed spit and choked. Despite tears forming, she gawked like a virginal teenager.

He rubbed his cheek as he stepped into the kitchen. The soft lighting kissed his face, enhancing the angle of his jaw and his wide lips. "What's wrong, sweetheart?"

Sugarplums. What can I say? Thoughts of making love to you plague me? No, I can't say that. Scaredy cat. She giggled. "I...I can't sleep." Then nodded at her excellent recovery.

He captured her hand and tugged her into a hug, pressing her cheek against his pec. She slumped, snuggling into his warm, velvety embrace. She was lost, truly. No way could she resist this amount of temptation, and it was downright unfair to ask her to. Exhaustion burned behind her eyes, but her thoughts zinged like a pinball machine on a sugar high.

"We can watch a movie if you want?"

She shook her head, rubbing her temple across his skin. "I... Why do you flirt with me?" *Holy sugar.* Not what she meant to say. She tried to pull away, lowering her chin to hide her burning face.

He held onto her. "I like you."

His voice reverberated in her ear. He liked her? Mm, what did that mean? "I like you too, that doesn't explain—"

"As in I want to date you for real, Blue." He tightened his arms, crushing her against him.

"What?" She whipped her head up to meet his gaze. "But...Antony? Fake kissing? Dinner and dancing?" She offered him what she hoped was a teasing smile. "Oli, are you joking with me?"

"Fake kissing? Is there such a thing?" He dipped his head to brush his lips across hers. "I do love kissing you." He hummed his pleasure before he captured her mouth for a searing kiss.

Her ears warmed as she melted, clinging to him like a historical romance cover model. He scrambled her thoughts with flicks of his tongue. Oh, she was a goner. A stern voice pushed through lust's haze. *This is Oli.*

She moaned. *Sure is. Gorgeous, sexy-as-chocolate Oliver Trent, my childhood friend.* The way her lady bits twanged said she didn't care who he was. But she *should* care. Breaking the kiss took all her concentration.

She held four fingers to her tingling lips while blinking at him. "I—"

"It's not your style to overthink this. It's simple, Blue. I find you incredibly attractive, know you inside and out, adore your sweet personality, and want to fuck you hard..." He ran his gaze over her face and lower to her heaving bosom.

Butterflies exploded through her chest. She held her palm to her cheek. "You didn't just say that, Oli."

He grinned. "What? How does that compare to your steamy questions? Did I imagine spanking your ass? You bet I did. Was I in agony when we discussed blowjobs? Yup."

She gaped. Not once had she thought he'd find her research arousing. "I'm sorry. I shouldn't have bothered you."

"Yes, you should have, and I'm glad you did. It got me off my ass and here in Colefield."

She squeaked, thumping his chest with a fist. "What? You returned for me? For sex?"

He laughed and gathered her close, his hands scorching her through the thin fabric of the sleep shirt. "I always planned to come home, Blue." He pressed and held his lips to her temple. Against her skin, he mumbled, "Now, put me out of my misery and agree to date me...for real."

"What about Antony?" She fought the urge to roll her eyes. Like that man could compare to Oli. Still, she wanted this Antony-misunderstanding cleared up. "I mean, I doubt—"

"If he plays ball, I'll step aside."

No, that felt wrong. She wanted a man to fight for her, to demand she choose him. Giving any man uncontested access to Blue coiled darkness in the pit of her stomach. "Just like that?" Well, she couldn't ask Oli to be hers forever, could she?

"It will kill me, Blue. I won't lie." He leaned back to cup her cheeks. "Just being with you and not doing what I long to do is killing me. But you're right. Antony was our initial goal. Let's finish this and see where we stand?"

She nodded, but what she wanted to do was run her lips down Oli's chest. Her fingers twitched to peel his yoga pants passed his hips. She ached to tilt her head and capture a taut nipple in her mouth. *See where we stand?* "We're in my kitchen in nothing but our pajamas, Oli. That's where we stand."

He groaned, his hands trembling when he slid them down her neck to grip her shoulders. "Don't tempt me, sweetheart." He spun her to face the passage. "Bed for you. Tomorrow, we'll visit your mom. I'll treat you to lunch afterwards."

"Lunch and dinner on the same day?" She smiled. "How lucky could one girl get?"

"Luckier if she doesn't save us both." He swatted her backside, sending her hurrying to her bedroom.

She huffed as she closed the door on his intense gaze. Sugar-honey-iced-tea, she was in a heap of trouble. It wasn't Antony's hands she dreamed touched her in her most sensitive places. Nor was it Antony who kissed her senseless, skittered excitement along her skin, and curled her toes with each caress. Oh, for sugar's sake, was she in love with Oli?

She threw herself onto the bed, yanked a pillow over her head, and screamed into the mattress. This was so bad. Sure, she wanted Oli to pin her to the bed and give new meaning to the word 'ravished.' But for how long would this last? She tossed the pillow aside, rolled onto her back, and stared at the ceiling. What was she going to do?

Heat unfurled in her core, and she pinched her thighs together, trying to hold back the aching need. She knew what her body wanted. Now to figure out where her heart stood on the matter. Loving him added a new dimension to this. She wouldn't have sex with him without some emotional involvement from his side. If she was going to risk their friendship, she wanted some guarantees.

Running her hand over her belly to the curls at the juncture of her thighs, she rubbed a finger between her lips and smothered a moan. With consistent twirls of a forefinger, she arched, her breathless whimpers slipping past her defenses as she climbed the ecstasy mountain.

"Night, Blue." Oli's voice penetrated the wooden door.

She squeaked and bit her bottom lip but didn't still her fingers rushing her to a delicious orgasm. Excitement scattered her heartbeat, that he was so close, could open the door at any moment, could stride in and finish her off. At the image of him thrusting into her, a wave of warmth and pleasure slammed across her body, dragging a moan from her. She trembled and shuddered, savoring each delicious tendril of warmth flooding her limbs.

"Blue." Something thumped against her door. "Please don't play with yourself. I'm trying to be strong here."

"Night, Oli," she managed, her voice too husky post-orgasm.

"Fuck." Another thump rattled the door. "You came already?"

She didn't answer but bolted for the bathroom to wash her hands. Did she feel guilty about her self-stimulation? No. She grinned at her flushed face. Nothing stopped him from doing the same, and if he thought of her, even better.

She snuck up to her door, expecting him to charge into her room. Silence reigned, so she crawled onto her bed, gathered her pillow into a hug, and drifted off.

~*~

"Morning." Blue had the audacity to smile as she waltzed into the kitchen. Her dark-gray leggings hugged her ass, and her baggy shirt hung off a bare shoulder.

Oliver scowled, nursing a strong, black coffee.

She danced around him, pouring herself a cup. "Breakfast?"

He shook his head, not daring to look at her again. She'd orgasmed with him on the other side of the door. Didn't she know what that did to a man? He'd taken care of his hard-on, but desire still burned along his veins. His orgasm had been swift and lackluster, feeding his need for her even more. His hand no longer satisfied and, if he was honest, hadn't for a while. Only so many visions and fantasies of Blue could carry him through. Now that he'd tasted her sweet lips, he needed the real thing to ease the ache in his loins.

The fool he was had agreed to step aside if Antony showed interest. Oliver was trusting his instincts, praying Antony wasn't a rival. The thing was, if he had said to hell with Antony, that she was Oliver's, it might have pushed her away. Shit, what to do? His silly plan to woo her had fallen flat and trapped him. Tonight was the dinner, tomorrow dancing. He was clinging to both as a lifeline. If he had his way, she would be in bed now, naked, her legs wrapped around his hips. Instead, he had to play nice.

He wasn't feeling...*nice*.

Blue's face came into his line of vision.

He blinked, belatedly realizing she'd said something. "What?"

"I said..." She lowered her voice. "You don't have to come with me this morning if you're not up to it."

"Oh, I'm definitely up." And as fucking hard as granite.

"Good," she snapped, grabbed an apple and bit into it. Arching a brow at him, she chewed while pulling a jacket on. "Someone's a little grumpy this morning."

He leapt off the stool and faced her. "Grumpy?"

She chuckled. "Did you and your hand have an argument?"

"Oh!" His breath rushed out of his lungs. "Why, you little..."

On a breathless laugh, she bolted for the SUV. His blood pumped through his veins, racing his heartbeat. He caught her just as she reached the driver door. Pinning her with his hips, he cupped her cheeks and held her still. Gazing deep into her eyes, he let himself drift away, sinking into her warmth. His focus shifted to her mouth.

Last night, rum had coated her tongue. This morning, she'd taste of apple. "Blue," he rasped.

"Oli." She smiled. "Why are we whispering?"

Her teasing engulfed his chest with heat, like the rising crescendo in an orchestral piece, a wave crashing onto shore. How he loved this woman. "I'm—"

"Full of nonsense, that's for sure." She thrust forward with her hips, forcing him back.

He winced when she brushed across his hard-on, but instead of climbing into the SUV, he stood there, watching her while she unplugged it from the wall. He'd been a breath away from confessing his love. *Double fuck*. He had to do it soon before the words tumbled from his lips at an inopportune time.

From inside the SUV, she tapped the windscreen, arching a brow.

He slid into the car and placed his hand on her thigh. When she didn't start the engine, he met her gaze while squeezing her leg. Her cheeks flushed a delicate pink. Without a word, she turned the key and reversed out of the garage.

The drive to the retirement village was in silence. He preferred it that way. Every time he drew a circle with his thumb, her leg would twitch and her breath hitch.

Was he playing dirty? Hell yes, but all was fair in love and war. Since he'd decided to pursue her, he'd do everything and anything to convince her she was his. Except for one small problem. He wanted her now, this instant. The idea of waiting another minute was sheer torture.

If he'd just wanted sex, last night would've sealed her fate.

He needed her heart to ache for him. For so many years, he'd yearned for her. He couldn't settle for less. Her thigh shifting from under his hand snapped him out of his thoughts.

Sprawled before him was the Haven Retirement Village—a compact one-level building with a partially covered courtyard, a conservatory, and a heated pool. Gray had shown Oliver the brochure. Not that there were many options in Colefield. Still, the facilities listed were that of a luxury resort and as expensive.

"Thailand has these amazing retirement villages. Many people are relocating their loved ones there."

"What?" She gasped. "Abandon their parents? Why would someone do that?"

"Something about how elderly-centric Thailand is. They offer the best care as if your loved ones are theirs." He captured her hand and curled it against his chest and ushered her along the walkway. "The weather is sub-tropical. No more cold winters affecting joints."

"Sounds like a discussion you had with your dad." Blue snuggled against him, then hurried ahead when he held the glass door open for her.

Light streamed in through large triple-pane windows, bathing the pale wainscotting and cream floor tiles with welcoming warmth. Chunky brown leather chairs with geometric cushions in a kaleidoscope of colors added joy. Abstract paintings dominated the walls.

Blue marched toward the reception counter. "I'll check us in. Mom's room is the eighth door on the right." She gestured to a hallway leading off on the left.

He shoved his hands in his pockets and strolled past nurses and pajama-clad residents toddling back and forth. At the number eight in brass, he knocked on the gaping door and peeked inside.

"Eddie?"

At the use of his dad's name, Oliver blinked at the woman—an older version of Navy. Seated in a chair in front of the window, she'd twisted to study him, her knuckles white where she gripped the chair. Gone was the vibrant woman he'd once called Aunt Lori.

Her room held a single bed, a nightstand, and a chair. Built in cupboards maximized the small space. The joyful colors of the linen and cushions did much to brighten the austere cream walls and lackluster blinds.

He opened his mouth to correct her, but Navy leaning against the wall outside the room shook her head. "Hi, L-Lorraine." It felt odd to be calling the older woman by her name without the respectful title of aunt.

Her beige cropped pants and baby-pink blouse were in her usual style—one she hadn't changed in years if his memories were correct.

Lori staggered to her feet and crossed to clasp Oliver's hand. "What are you doing here? Matt mustn't see you."

Blue's eyes widened, and she slunk farther away, just in case Lori spotted her. He stepped toward her, but she rolled her hand, urging him to continue the strange conversation with Lori.

Despite a frown forming, he forced a smile. "You look...lovely, Lorraine."

She huffed. "It's your smooth tongue that got us into trouble. Matt must never find out."

Blue paled and pressed four fingers to her gaping mouth.

"Find out what?" What was Aunt Lori going on about? Oliver settled her into her chair, pausing to drape a blanket over her lap.

She blushed. "You know. The kiss...and what followed afterward. I meant to tell you so many times." She released a shuddering breath. "Gray's yours."

Blue gasped from the hallway.

Ice drenched Oliver from the tips of his ears to his toes. Gray was his half-brother? "How can you be sure, Lorraine?" He croaked the question, but he had to be certain.

"Timing." Lori tapped her nose. Something through the window snagged her attention, and her eyes glazed over. She hummed a haunting tune while picking at the knots in her crocheted blanket.

He kissed her temple and crept out, finding a crying Navy pacing outside.

She threw herself into his arms, burying her face in the curve of his neck. "It can't be true, Oli."

"We can do a DNA test." He rubbed her back, cradling her closer. "But should we, Blue?"

She leaned back and sniffed. "*I* want to know." Wiping her cheeks, she tried to smile, but the tears still flowed.

Shock rolled over him in waves. No, he must have misheard. Maybe they both had. "This will kill my dad."

"Shit, Oli, what are we going to do? What about Gray?" She captured his hands for a squeeze.

Her presence lessened the vise crushing his chest. He drew in a shaky breath. "Visit with your mom. I'll wait here, and maybe when you're done, I'll have a plan."

She pressed a kiss to his knuckles and disappeared inside Lori's room. He leaned against the wall, his knees weakening. What the fuck? His mind reeled. His emotions swung on a pendulum, not pausing long enough for him to focus.

What if it wasn't true, but what if it was? Should they reveal this?

Anger swelled, trembling his body. Pops had cheated on Mom, on Oliver. Such an action impacted the family. Regardless of Lori not telling Pops about Gray, it didn't excuse their reckless behavior.

Oliver gritted his teeth. A weight settled on his shoulders like an anvil. Pops would be arriving in a few days. Should he confront him? Should he and Blue keep this to themselves?

Fuck.

He didn't know what to do, and the way Blue looked to him for guidance tore at him. Whatever they decided, he vowed, wouldn't hurt her further. If he had his way, she would be his forever. Her happiness mattered, and he would make damn sure she felt nothing but cherished.

Chapter Ten

Lunch was in silence and with good reason. Navy couldn't bring herself to eat, not with the knot twisting her stomach and radiating pain outward. Her mother had had an affair. Possibly. Unconfirmed. And if she had, and Gray was the by-blow, how did that change their family dynamics? He'd been there for Navy throughout her life, so that bond remained regardless of the DNA results. And he was best friends with Oli. Knowing Gray's true parentage wouldn't change that. The only person this would truly affect was Eddie. He'd be devastated Mom had lied to him all these years.

For the first time, Navy was grateful Dad wasn't alive to learn this.

Her breath whooshed out. She twirled pasta on her fork, let it unravel, then repeated the process. Oli cut his pork chop into bite-sized pieces he didn't eat.

"Mom must have taken one look at you and believed you to be Eddie." Navy frowned, sifting through her memories of old photos. Had younger Eddie looked like Oli? Gray did have gray eyes just like Eddie's. She'd always thought that a coincidence.

"Mm, you might be right." Oli paired his knife and fork in the center of his plate. He wrapped his long fingers around his tumbler of whisky on ice and threw it back, gesturing to the waiter for another.

Navy sighed. She wanted nothing more than to drown her tumultuous emotions with wine, but she still had bread to bake before dinner. At least, she'd stopped crying. Logically, Gray's parentage was just a shock. The real dilemma was whether to tell him.

"Should we—?

"We have time to decide before he arrives...I hope." He offered her a smile, shoved the breadbasket aside, and clasped her hand.

She clung to him, needing his strength. "Hope he visits or hope we have time?" She released his hand long enough to ask for a whisky too. Just one should be fine, right?

"Both." He squeezed her hand and pulled away when Milly reached their table. "I'll drop you off. I need to meet the deliverers at the lodge."

"On a Sunday?" Navy arched a brow, then shrugged. "Fine by me. I have to bake bread for Milly's."

He studied her over his whisky glass, his eyes narrowing. "Dinner at six?"

The air thickened between them. A wave of goosebumps trickled down her back. "Six."

"Dinner date for real, Blue."

She forced a chuckle, trying to hide her scattered senses. "Are you hoping for a goodbye kiss?"

His nostrils flared when he sucked in a deep breath. "I get kisses anyway." He didn't dip his gaze to her pebbled nipples. She'd give him credit for that.

"You're taking liberties, Mr. Trent."

He grinned. "I am."

She fanned her face with the paper napkin, the flush of whisky and desire tying her tongue. Her writer's mind reeled, though, so she grabbed her phone to best capture what he made her feel.

"Using me as research?"

She hummed a yes while listing her symptoms.

"I dreamed of you reading my favorite scenes to me."

Her head whipped up. "You did?"

"All I had was your voice, Blue, asking me questions that would make a sex therapist blush."

She nibbled on the inside of her cheek while placing the phone face down on the table. "I said I was sorry."

"Are you? Should you be?" He snatched her hand and brought her fingers to his lips. "I don't want an apology." His breath warmed her skin.

A question plagued her, and despite her clamoring instincts warning her not to ask, the words tumbled free. "What *do* you want?"

His eyelashes fluttered, a sensual smile pursed his lips, and his gaze narrowed on her mouth. "You."

Right then, her insides pooled into a liquid fire. She pinned her thighs together and willed herself to look away. But she couldn't. His magnetism snagged her like a deer in headlights.

"Sex could ruin our relationship." She winced but couldn't deny the consequences would be devastating if they pursued this.

He shook his head. "You think this is just sex?" He nipped a fingertip, and the frisson of fire traveling down her arm drew a gasp from her. Then with infinite care, he pressed a kiss to her skin as if to apologize.

"If it's not, then what is it?"

With his gaze boring into hers, he lowered her hand but didn't release it. He ran his thumb over her knuckles, eliciting another shiver. "It's light, magic, sweetness, promise, and joy."

"Oliver," she huffed. "You just described an orgasm."

He laughed. "It's more, Blue. I could reveal all, but I'm not ready yet." He waved at Milly to bring the check. "Neither are you."

She scowled. *What the hell did that mean?* "Cryptic much?"

"Trust me, please."

At his earnest pleading, she nodded. "How do you want me to dress for dinner?"

His focus shifted, but he raised his gaze, his mouth parting. "Can I say come naked?"

Holy sugar, is it hot in here? Claiming back her hand, she gulped down her drink, relishing the chill of the ice and the burn of the whisky. "Oli, be serious."

"Oh, I'm deadly serious when it comes to you, Blue." The gaze he leveled on her confirmed his words. "Dinner's at The Brazen Horse."

This situation was so out of control and beyond her experiences. She wanted to tease him in return, to flirt as Hannah would have. Hell, this was worse than with Antony. How had this happened? One moment they were playing a game to woo a man she couldn't give a sugar about. The next, the sexual tension between her and Oli had shot through the roof.

After he paid, he rose, circled her chair, and held open her jacket. She slid into it, her skin prickling where his fingers touched: at the nape of her neck, on her cheek, and along her collarbone when he came around to zip her closed.

She mumbled her thanks and allowed him to lace his fingers through hers. Aware of the interest the townsfolk frequenting Milly's showed them, she ducked her head and crowded Oli. He released her hand and drew her against him, throwing his arm across her shoulders.

"They think we're doing *it*," she whispered, slicing a glance at the faces turned their way.

"No matter who you date, Blue, they'll be watching, judging." He held out his hand, asking for the car keys.

She dug them out of her jacket and dropped them into his palm. When he opened the passenger door for her, she paused to meet his gaze. The vibe had changed to something serious like they were on a precipice. What lay below and ahead she couldn't fathom. She scrambled for a way to bring back their playful banter.

Cocking her head and forcing a smile, she hoped to appear as sophisticated as the women he was used to. "How about a kiss to give them something to talk about?"

He stilled, studied her face, then cupped her cheek, running his thumb along her bottom lip. "Don't tempt me."

Mortification fired her cheeks, making her eyes water, but she persevered with a chuckle. "Little me tempting you?" She nuzzled his hand.

"Blue," he rasped.

She shrugged, giving up on trying to charm him, and climbed into the car. "Thought you wanted a public kiss."

He blinked at her, hesitating to close the door. She smothered a smile. Maybe she could fluster him even if she lacked the skill of flirting. Something unraveled deep within her at how easily she affected him. Her breath locked in her chest while Oli circled the hood of her SUV.

As soon as he settled in the seat, she placed her hand on his thigh and squeezed.

He tensed, then twisted to level a heated gaze on her. "You're playing with fire, Blue."

She snorted. "What are you going to do about it, Oli?" Her inner girl squealed at the rush of power drowning her inhibitions.

He growled, "Do you have any idea how much I want you?" He started the engine and reversed. "Will you spread those thighs and let me fuck you?

Her heartbeat did the Tango. A wave of need traveled from her chest to her core and coiled there.

"Or would you prefer to see where this leads?"

She wanted to say both, but the way he gripped and released the steering wheel gave her pause. He struggled with something that held him back. "Very well, Oli, we'll do it your way."

"My way?" He pursed his lips and steered the car onto her road. "That's dirty fighting putting the decision on me."

He was right. She drew her hand back and twisted within the confines of the seatbelt to face him.

"Let me be honest here." She sucked in a ragged breath, gathering what courage the whisky lent her. "I don't 'spread my thighs' for anyone. If we're to risk our relationship, then I need some sort of guarantee we're not ruining what we have."

He pulled the SUV to a halt outside her house and kept the engine running. "Life doesn't come with guarantees. You have to decide what you're willing to risk or life will choose the sacrifice for you."

Pain cinched her chest, shooting out in pulses. "I can't *risk* losing you, Oli."

"And I don't want to stay the way we are." He put the gear in park and hopped out of the car, circling the hood to open her door.

Stunned, she let him usher her up the driveway, but when they neared the garage door, he spun her and pinned her to the wall. Without hesitation, he sliced his mouth across hers, tossing her thoughts wild. She succumbed to his warm, soft lips, reveled in the swooping of his tongue, and in the sheer, masculine taste of him.

Too soon, he broke the kiss and rested his temple on hers as he fought for air. "I need you too much, Blue." His hand shook where he brushed hair off her cheek. "Dinner for real?"

She nodded, too tongue-tied to speak a word. Dazed, she watched him jog to her SUV and drive off. While heading for the kitchen, she removed her jacket to start on the dozens of loaves promised to Milly's. On autopilot, she kneaded dough, and while she waited for it to rise, she baked cupcakes and apple pie, her thoughts swinging from a life with or without Oli, and what she'd wear tonight. When the bread dough was twice its size, she lined the pans, then filled and slotted them into the industrial ovens.

She still trembled, and indecision flitted her from one outcome to another. Tina would tell her to risk it all for love, like she had with Lisa. Navy wasn't so brave. Parts of her—well, eighty-seven percent if she was being honest—wanted Oli to be with her forever. She *loved* him, more now than before. Loved him like a man, not just as her oldest friend.

The way a sensual smile curled his lips when he looked at her.

How he supported her no matter what she did. Whether it was making decadent cupcakes or writing sex scenes in the middle of lunch.

He knew her so well, she couldn't hide her motives, thoughts, and reactions from him.

And holy sugar, he was handsome with his blond locks cascading over those hazel eyes.

A thought pinged across her subconscious that he'd moved home for her. He'd committed himself before knowing how she felt or whether she could see him in a romantic light. He'd risked much.

The thump of a car door snapped her out of her daze. A glance at the clock confirmed her worst nightmare. She was late. The final batch of bread baked in the ovens. She couldn't go to dinner until they were done.

Drying her hands after washing pans, she tossed the towel on the counter, readying to bolt down the passage to her room. A knock at the front door halted her. She frowned. Oli would've strolled right in.

She flung the door open and blinked at the man standing on her doorstep. "Antony?"

He offered her a sheepish smile. "Hi, Navy, sorry to drop in like this."

Her manners kicked in, and she gestured for him to come in. Closing the door behind him, she frowned at his back. "Do sit. Coffee?"

"Please." He drew in a deep breath and smiled. "Smells divine. I love your cupcakes."

"I just made a dozen, want one with your coffee?" She circled the island to the coffee machine.

"I won't say no." He chose Oli's favorite spot but didn't lean back. Instead, he rested his elbows on his knees when he squatted on the edge of the seat.

She snuck glances as she made them each a coffee. What the hell was Antony doing in her living room? He seemed nervous, his knee bouncing while he studied her home. He looked good too, in skinny jeans and a black T-shirt beneath his windbreaker.

"I'm sorry. I forgot to take your jacket." She pointed at the hooks on the wall. "Help yourself."

He leapt to his feet, sliding his jacket off to expose muscles she'd ogled for months. A flock of sparrows was tattooed on his wrist. She hadn't noticed that before.

After serving him coffee and a cupcake, she settled on her side of the couch. A twang of guilt sliced through her curiosity. Being this close to Antony when she loved Oli swirled her thoughts on how Oli would react when he came home. And he would, soon, but she couldn't chase Antony out. Her mother had raised her better than that.

When Antony moaned over her cupcake, she shifted, finding his reaction awkward. Yup, as she'd guessed. She'd liked the idea of him and not the man, per se. After all, she knew nothing about him and hadn't taken the time to find out. That said it all.

While he sipped his coffee, he studied her, reminding her that baking detritus covered her clothes. Her skin was clammy too from the heat of the ovens and the hours spent kneading and washing.

"Where's your friend?" He scanned the room like she'd hidden Oli in the shadows.

"His stuff arrived today. He'll be here soon. We're going out to dinner tonight." She bit her lip, having revealed too much. Pfft, Colefield was a small town.

"About dinner, I...er, wanted to ask you out."

She unfolded her legs and inched forward to place her half-drunk coffee on the table. "Dinner?" She frowned. "Why now?" *Maybe Oli had been right? Men want what other men have.*

"Been meaning to ask you for months. Just couldn't find the courage. And with your friend in town—"

"You thought you'd better get in on the action?" Anger flared, stiffening her body. The urge to hit him gripped her.

He winced. "Not how I would've put it, but yes."

She wanted to scream she wasn't free until Christmas, but townsfolk knew everything about everyone. Despite kind of getting the dinner invitation she'd yearned for, what pulsed through her body was irritation. She liked him better from afar. "Wednesday's my only free night. I'm sure you've heard by now that Oli and I are dating."

"Yeah, dinner and dancing." A pulse ticked at the base of Antony's jaw. "The Brazen Horse, Club Frozen?"

"Since the restaurant and the nightclub are the only ones in town, then yes." She rose to her feet and glowered at him. "Planning on stalking me?"

"Like you said, the only restaurant and club in town." He smiled. "All's fair in war, right?"

She gritted her teeth. With Tammy as hostess at The Brazen Horse and Antony lurking at its bar, tonight promised to be epic.

Chapter Eleven

Oliver frowned at the SUV hogging the driveway. With them leaving for dinner soon, he didn't want to block the visitor who'd parked close to the door. A flurry of snow had begun, promising a dip in temperatures. He studied the distance between him and the front door, analyzing whether Blue might catch a chill.

His body ached after unpacking his belongings from the van into his new home. He'd stacked everything inside without bothering to place furniture. When construction began, he'd have to move his things anyway. The exertion had done much to calm the lust coursing through his body and solidified his determination to woo Blue. She was right to be nervous about risking their relationship. Yet, he was done waiting and yearning with things not progressing between them. Tonight, he hoped to reach second base.

She had at least agreed to date him for real.

He opened the front door and froze. *What the fuck?* Adrenaline exploded through him, tightening his grip on the door handle. Antony faced Oliver, a coffee in his hand. On the table sat an empty plate. If Blue didn't look fuming mad, Oliver might have revealed the jealousy demanding he challenge the man to a duel.

"Oli, I'm running late. The last batch's in the ovens." She strode to the hooks and offered Antony his jacket, her message clear. Especially when she snapped his jacket at him like he was the bull and she the matador.

Oliver captured her chin between forefinger and thumb to give her a quick kiss. "I'm running late too, sweetheart."

Her cheeks flushed a beautiful peach when she rasped, "Good. Antony was just leaving."

The man nodded, took his jacket, and while slipping it on, he met her gaze. "Wednesday?"

She huffed. "I'll think about it, but don't get your hopes up."

Oliver stepped aside to let Antony pass, but it took everything within him to smother a triumphant grin when she slammed the door and cursed a blue streak in flowery baking terms.

"What just happened?"

She paused mid-tirade. "He asked me out *to get in on the action.*"

An alarm rang, and she bolted for the kitchen, pulling trays from the ovens and setting them to the side. Yanking oven mitts off, she gestured to her stained shirt. "Let me get ready."

He waited for her bedroom door to close before he whooped and fist-pumped the air. *Hallelujah.* He marched to his room, disrobed, and jumped into the shower, excitement skittering along his skin. How pissed off Blue was with Antony bolstered Oliver's image. Sure, the same jealousy that Ronnie had inspired had reared its green head, but Oliver liked to think he was older, wiser...better equipped to deal with what Blue invoked within him.

He donned gunmetal-gray slacks, a crisp white-collared shirt—with a few buttons left undone, and a dark-gray jacket—its tailored shoulders enhanced his. He ran his hands through his hair until he'd achieved the perfect just-woke-up look, brushed his teeth, and finished with black polished dress shoes over matching socks. After a splash of cologne on his five o'clock shadow, he was out the door and striding to the kitchen.

Blue wasn't waiting in the living room. He shrugged on his coat to park the SUV closer to the house, returning minutes later to find she hadn't made an appearance yet. Striding down the passage to her door, he half expected it to open before he reached it.

"Blue?" He rested his temple on the door.

"Oh, Oli, I can't decide." She huffed. "I'm so angry with this whole Antony-thing, I'm tempted to throw caution to the wind."

He gripped the door handle. "Are you decent?"

"Yeah, kind of."

Entering her room, he wasn't prepared for the vision before him. His breath hitched. Wild horses couldn't have stopped his gaze from traversing and memorizing every inch of her.

"Is your silence good? Is this too much?" She gestured to the deep 'V' of her red, kimono-style, semi-transparent blouse draping over her lovingly-encased-in-black-lace breasts. A wide corset-like black leather belt cinched her waist in, creating a frill with the edges of her shirt. Black pleated slacks hugged her hips and ass, ending at red pumps adding a few inches to her height.

"You know what they say about women in red shoes." He grinned, willing his heartbeat to calm despite his focus snagging on her cleavage. Holy fuck, he wanted to nuzzle her and press a kiss to each breast.

"What?" She faced the mirror to pin her hair back on one side, exposing the delicate shell of an ear. She looped dangling earrings in, so long they brushed her collarbones.

"Red shoes mean no underwear." His gaze dipped to her backside, searching for the telltale lines of her panties. Heat exploded from his chest to his groin at not finding any. His fingers twitched with the urge to confirm his suspicions.

"Since you can see my bra..." She rested her hands on her hips and studied her reflection in the mirrors lining her built-in cupboards. "This is insane. I should change."

He closed the distance between them to grasp her shoulders and layer her back against his front. "You look stunning, Navy." He met her gaze in the mirror and rested his chin on her shoulder, drawing in a deep whiff of her perfume. "Maybe we can skip dinner? Go straight to dessert?" He slipped his arms around her waist and crushed her against him.

Her eyes widened, and she wiggled her ass. Her mouth parted on a gasp, and she slowed her movements across his hard cock. "I *am* tempted."

Her sensuous jiggle was almost his undoing. He brushed his lips along the curve of her neck to her ear to nip the lobe. "But you want to prove a point."

She trembled in his arms when she stepped away and faced him. "No man dates me just because another man's interested. Do you know what he said? That he'd been meaning to ask me out for months." She stomped her foot. "What would have happened had you not pretended to date me, Oli? How long would it have taken him to ask?" She tossed a glance at the mirror then ran her hands over her hips. "A girl's got to have some pride."

"So you want to show him what he'll never have?" Fuck, Oliver hoped so.

She met his gaze. "Is that petty of me?" She gazed at the mirror and pouted. "It is. I should change."

He cupped her throat, sliding his hand up to bury his fingers in her hair and press his thumb to her cheek. Wrapping his arm around her waist again, he pinned her back to his chest while directing her mouth to his. Her erratic pulse beat against his palm.

He cradled her, her breath warming his chin as he met her gaze to drown in the blue depths. "You're beautiful, Blue." Brushing his lips across hers, he didn't break eye contact, even when he deepened the kiss, swiping his tongue across hers.

With a moan, she dug her nails into his forearm and kissed him back. His control quaked under her onslaught. She gripped his hand clasping her cheek and guided it down to cup her breast. Fire scorched his fingers, enhanced by the silkiness of her blouse, and the swollen plumpness of her breast under his touch. Her nipple puckered in his palm. He squeezed, massaged, and rubbed, relishing every gasp his reverence earned.

She drew away, her breathing ragged. "A goodbye kiss."

His heart froze. "What?"

She pulled on his hand, freeing her breast, and kissed his fingertips. "This way we don't have to be nervous about the after-dinner kiss."

He harumphed. "If you keep tormenting me like this, you'll get more than a kiss." He brushed a curl off her cheek. "Ready?"

Food was the last thing he wanted, but she did look sexy as all hell. The urge to rub Antony's face in Oliver's conquest was too irresistible. Here he'd thought the man wasn't interested. Turned out, he was wrong. Had he not ramped his seduction, who knows how Blue would've responded.

She applied lip gloss, grabbed her black clutch, and strode down the passage to the coat hooks. He trailed her, adjusting his hard-on in his tailored slacks. Tonight couldn't be worse than sleeping in the mosquito-infested swamps of Botswana. Since he'd endured that, he'd endeavor to survive dinner until home time.

Instead of her usual jacket, she slipped on a knee-length black coat that cinched in at the waist. He smiled. The more time he spent with her, the more he realized why she owned his heart. He offered his elbow. She hooked her arm through and clasped his forearm. Without another word, he ushered her to the car, opening the passenger door for her.

"What do you feel like for dinner?" he asked when he slid into the driver's seat.

"Mm, my usual." She grinned.

"And that is?" He paused with his hand on the keys in the ignition.

"Tagliatelle bacon carbonara." She frowned when he didn't start the engine. "What's the matter?"

"Your hand should be where, Ms. Sanders?"

A blush bloomed on her cheeks, and she hurriedly placed her hand on his thigh. "My apologies, Mr. Trent, but I do believe you said I was playing with fire."

"I did, and you are, but I like your touch." He chuckled and reversed down the driveway. "Bacon in anything sounds perfect. Their steak's amazing if I remember correctly."

"Oh, yes, and you may need your stamina tonight. By all means, carbo load."

His breath caught. He sliced a glance at her, tightening his grip on the steering wheel. The promise of an orgasmic evening thickened the tension between them. He twitched when she scraped her nails to his knee then down his thigh again.

"Did you decide, sweetheart? What has changed since this afternoon?"

She sighed and stared through the window at the snowfall. "Antony's unexpected dinner invitation. I like you far more than any man I know."

"Like?" He smiled. "You *love* me."

She chuckled. "I do. Lust you too."

"Ditto, with every ounce of my being." If only she realized he was *in love* with her.

"Aw, Mr. Trent, there you go being all romantic and such. Be still my poor heart." She fluttered her fingers above her left breast, snagging his attention.

He blinked. Thankfully, he'd stopped at a traffic light and could admire the play of golden lamplight and silver moonlight across her cleavage.

"It's green," she whispered while giving his thigh a squeeze.

He met her gaze and smiled. Without saying a word, he pulled off, driving the car the last leg of their trip. The restaurant's lights glowed warm and welcoming through the windows. Patrons chatted at their tables, smiles and hand gestures animating their enjoyment. As soon as he parked, he loped around the hood to plug the SUV in then opened her door. Grasping her offered hand, he brought her fingers to his lips for a kiss.

"Ready to amaze?" He grinned.

She drew in a long breath, captured his hand holding hers, and pressed a kiss to his knuckles. "Thank you."

"For what?" He ushered her onto the salted sidewalk, closed the car door, and offered her an elbow. His chest puffed up, like he had a hand in creating this beautiful woman beside him.

She looped her arm through the crook, grabbed his bicep with her other hand, and snuggled against him. "For everything. You didn't have to be my research partner, buy a lodge, and move home, or help me make an idiot jealous."

He paused, meeting her gaze. "Yes, I did." He cupped her cheek, stroking his thumb just under her bottom lip. "And one day soon, I hope to share my reasons."

Her eyebrow rose. "Intriguing."

"No nagging like you did every birthday and Christmas. I won't share until it's time."

"Nag? Me? I'd never..." She laughed, but it dwindled. "I'm always ready to listen, Oli. Whatever you need."

He snorted. Whatever he needed? It wasn't dinner, that's for damn sure. Before he succumbed, bundled her into the car, and took her home for a long-overdue ravishment, he escorted her into the restaurant. Pausing for effect, he gazed upon her with all the love she invoked, wanting the townsfolk to see what she could not.

That she owned his heart.

Chapter Twelve

Navy floated on a cloud. Oli's attentiveness and the desire in his eyes did much to ease her nervousness. Her hands twitched to cover herself when he removed her coat, exposing her risqué outfit. If he hadn't reacted mesmerized, she might have changed into something...less indecent, more...her.

She almost left, not wanting Tammy to take their coats. But the blonde's smile faltered, her gaze fixed on Navy's blouse.

"Table for two, please," Oli said. "Preferably by a window."

Tammy jerked back and dumped their coats into a nearby waiter's arms. "Certainly." She led them to a secluded table by a window a little too close to the bar. Her hips swayed as she stomped. She stopped and flicked her wrist at the table. "Cindy will be your waitress."

Navy blinked at Tammy's disappearing back. She frowned. "Was it something—?"

"She's jealous, Blue, and she should be. You're gorgeous...and mine." He pulled out a chair and waited for her to sit.

She did but in a daze. Had he said 'mine?' Her throat squeezed shut.

Tears burned at the backs of her eyes. A sense of peace settled in her soul while excitement danced like butterflies along her skin. Her gaze traveled over him when he seated himself opposite her and captured her hand in his.

"Wine? A cocktail?" He studied their clasped hands, running his thumb across her knuckles.

Her breath rushed out in a whoosh. She dipped her chin to hide her shock. She *loved* him, loved this man who'd been her friend for so long. Her chest swelled with hot, sticky emotions. Joy exploded like fireworks, but nerves tensed her muscles. Fear was swift to slither into her stomach. What if he didn't love her back? Sure, he'd asked to date for real, admitted to finding her sexy, and his hard-on from earlier proved it. Still, sex was a far cry from forever after.

"It's not a life or death decision, Blue." He chuckled.

Yes, it was. She'd never been in love. With Ronnie, it had been a crush. Sexually, there'd been two men she'd shared intimate but fleeting moments with. She poked her heart, checking that the burning sweetness saturating it was indeed love. What she'd once felt for Oli was brotherly love, something she could compare to her feelings for Gray. But this? Aching need, wild excitement claiming her thoughts, fantasies of his kisses becoming more, and underlining it...breathless, knee-weakening hope?

"White wine, please," she croaked.

Holy sugar, what was she going to do? If this was just sex, her heart would break. Yes, he'd claimed it was more, but how many men said that? She had to remember, Oli was a man first. He'd never lied to her, but not revealing Ronnie's nefarious plans proved he could hide his true motives. Maybe that's what he wanted to share with her when the time was right? His reasons behind this fake-turned-real dating.

"Are you all right, sweetheart?" He brought her hand to his lips for a kiss.

Sugar-honey-iced-tea, act cool. She tilted her head and smiled at him. "Just thirsty."

He released her hand and snagged a passing waiter, ordering a bottle of water for the table. A frown furrowed his brow. She trailed his gaze to where Antony sat at the bar. While Tammy spoke to him with violent arm gestures, he raised his beer to salute Navy. His focus shifted to her cleavage, and the urge to stuff her cloth napkin there gripped her.

Antony's perusal had her needing a bath and a good scrub. Oli's admiration inspired her sensuality.

Oli captured her hand again, drawing her gaze to his face. "We can skip dinner."

She squeezed his fingers. "And admit defeat? Never." She straightened and raised the menu, peering at him over the top. "Want to share dessert with me?"

"Depends." His voice deepened. "If you're on the menu, then yes."

Heat bloomed across her cheeks. She flipped the menu down, creating a short breeze to cool her. When Cindy arrived to pour water into their glasses, Navy tossed her a grateful smile.

"I'd like a bottle of Chardonnay or a Viognier." Oli flicked through the menu, no doubt searching for the wine list.

Cindy frowned. "I'm afraid we only have the house white wine—a sauvignon blanc."

He winced but nodded.

"A whisky on the rocks for him." Navy chuckled and waited for Cindy to scurry off. "Missing the big city?"

His eyes turned a lovely dove gray. Something intense swirled in their depths, snatching her breath. "No. I'm exactly where I've dreamed of being."

She trembled, questions burning her tongue. Grabbing the glass, she gulped the water. "Um...what's in the cards for the lodge?" The safest subject change she could think of.

"Construction begins when Pops arrives."

Which meant soon. "And what will you be doing?"

He didn't answer, just stared at her with a smirk curling his sinful mouth. "What else do you have planned...writing-wise?"

"Was thinking of starting a series about a group of friends in a small town, each finding love."

"A town like Colefield?" He tapped his chin, then leaned back when Cindy slid his whisky onto the table and poured the wine.

"Ready to order?" She tucked her tray under her arm.

"No starter for me, not when I want dessert," Navy said to Oli.

He pressed the tip of his tongue to his top lip. "Same," he rasped. "As discussed, Blue?"

She nodded, and he proceeded to order a medium-to-rare steak with a side salad, and for her, a tagliatelle bacon carbonara.

She continued the description of her proposed book. "Spinsters ranging from say the late twenties to on the cusp of forty? They might even be sisters. Eclectic characters with an annoying habit of getting into everyone's business. Was thinking of adding a century-old mystery in the family house. Maybe a letter, a painting." She shrugged. "I might start on it after Sugar Momma's opening day."

"I look forward to reading them." He winked at her while pouring more wine into her glass.

She fanned herself with the menu. "The eldest is having an affair with the mortician, another is stalking her neighbor—a man doing something suspicious at night." Navy laughed. "I'm making this up as we sit here."

He smiled, affection warming his once-again hazel eyes. "I never knew how talented you are, Blue. I should have realized. Your baking's sublime, and your writing's..." His gaze dipped lower for a second before he glanced up. "Evocative and imbued with sensuality."

Her face caught on fire, the heat traveling down her throat to her cleavage. Holy sugar, could Oli get any sexier? Did spontaneous human combustion exist? She dropped the menu and clasped the glass, needing the condensation from the chilled wine to cool her.

He reached across the table and tucked an escaped tendril behind her ear. "So...will you accept Antony's invitation?"

The air warmed around them as she gazed into Oli's eyes. "Um, probably not." She laughed. "Of course it's a no, Oli. I want someone who will bend over backward to date me. Waiting three months then tossing out a pathetic invitation? Pfft, not this woman. You and Gray raised me to expect better."

"We did?" A smile warmed his eyes.

"Yup, on how not to date. I'd call your string of girls Gray's or Oli's friend because I lost track of who you two were dating."

His lips thinned. "Yeah, that was until I dumped Tammy."

Navy paused. "That's right, but then we didn't dare mention Tammy's name. We thought you pined for her."

"Pined?" He grabbed his whisky and threw it back, waving the glass at the waitress. "No, I wasn't pining for Tammy."

"Oh." Navy shrugged. "Regardless, that's when you stopped the long procession of girls. Not sure what dating was like for you in the city."

A slow smile spread across his lips. "Is this the 'how many lovers came before you' discussion?"

She paused. Before her? Yes, sex was *so* going to happen tonight. She forced a chuckle while shaking her head. "I don't want to know."

He grinned. "You're right. Thinking about you with another man..." He curled his fingers into a fist where they rested on the tablecloth. His smile faltered.

Her breath caught. Was he jealous? She blinked, unsure whether it was joy or embarrassment exploding butterflies in her chest. Not that she knew what to say.

Cindy rescued Navy by placing a bowl of pasta with toasted and buttered ciabatta onto the table. "The bowl is hot," she warned, then smiled as she placed Oli's steak in front of him. "Anything else?"

"No, this is perfect." Navy beamed. As soon as they were alone again, she picked up her fork. "We need to discuss what my mom revealed."

Oli nodded as he slid a bite of steak and salad into his mouth.

"Did we decide to tell Gray?" She sprinkled parmesan, then twirled pasta onto her fork.

"Would you want to know? If it was you and not Gray?" Oli sipped his whisky before slicing into his steak again.

"Yes. Gray has a chance to build a closer relationship with Eddie. He's been like a father after Dad died anyway."

Oli grimaced. "Shit, I'll have to tell Pops."

"There's that too." She paused while chewing the creamiest pasta with salty bacon. "We can do it together."

"Perhaps we should talk to Gray first. Do a DNA test to confirm before we drag Pops into it."

She hummed on a sip of wine. "Wise. So, it will be our secret."

A smile curled his sexy mouth. She blinked, then lowered her gaze to save herself.

"We'll have to sit Gray down," he said. "You know how unfocussed he can be when not working."

She laughed. "I sure do. Mom had to redo the kitchen when he set it on fire making popcorn."

"Or the time he dominoed all the trees while buying a Christmas tree."

She chuckled. "Mr. Ferguson's horror was priceless."

Oli's laughter dwindled. "It feels so good to laugh...with you."

"Now that you're home, I'm sure there'll be new memories and laughter when Gray visits with more of his antics." She grinned. "It will almost be like old times."

"Almost." With a whisky in hand, Oli leaned back to study her. "How's your pasta?"

"Divine. Want a bite?" She twirled and raised the laden fork, cupping it with the spoon underneath, in case tendrils unraveled.

Obediently, he opened his mouth. "It *is* good," he moaned. "My turn." He set his glass aside to cut a piece of steak, choosing salad items with care.

"Steak is steak, Oli."

"Fair is fair, Blue." He held up his fork.

Sighing, she opened her mouth, but he froze. His eyes darkened. "Shit, Blue, you're so damn sexy," he rasped, then popped the perfect bite into her mouth before she could react.

She chewed under his scrutiny, unable to make a sound. The meat was succulent and delicious, deserving of a moan, but she didn't dare. "It's...good." What else could she say? *Take me now, on this table, in front of witnesses?* She huffed.

The clink of glass on glass snapped her out of her lewd thoughts. He topped up her wine, his knowing gaze fixed on her. The intensity in his eyes promised a night of bliss. She must be like a virgin to him, all aflutter under his masterful seduction.

A man from the city having dated all kinds of women? How can I compare?

"Oh, no, I know that look." He reached across the table. "Don't doubt this chemistry between us. Don't doubt my sincerity in wanting to date you."

She blinked back tears. "Am I that obvious?"

"Only to me, Blue."

She snorted, tempted to roll her eyes. "I'm not...*experienced.*"

He squeezed her hand. "It will be like riding a bike."

"Oli," she whined. "I haven't ridden a bike in years." She shuffled on her chair, trying to ease the renewed ache in her loins. "Shall we go?"

He jerked back. "But...I thought you wanted dessert?"

"When I make their cakes and pies?" She arched a brow. "Was thinking of eating a little lemon meringue pre-dawn."

His breath hitched, and he tightened his grip on her fingers. "I'm holding you to your word." Releasing her, he gestured to Cindy who hurried across.

Her eyes widened when he asked for the check. "Is something wrong?"

"Not at all. Just a little tired, is all." Navy stifled a fake-yawn.

While he paid, his gaze rested on her, his eyes twinkling. As soon as he pocketed his wallet, she rose, accepting her coat a waiter offered her. A glowering Tammy watched from beside Antony.

"And you can act," Oli whispered as he held open her coat. "That's the only thing you're faking tonight though." His lips brushed the shell of her ear, sending a shiver down her spine. With a kiss on her cheek, he shrugged on his jacket. "Ready?"

She looped her arm through his.

The freezing air hit her when she stepped into the night. Her breath escaped in puffs of condensation. Dark clouds obscured the moon. Oli gathered her close, tucking her against his side as he ushered her to the SUV.

Once again squeezing his thigh, his hand cupping hers, he drove in second gear, coasting through the green traffic lights at a steady speed. The heat poured off him, tempting her to snuggle closer. She tried not to glance his way, not with the massive bulge in his pants stealing her ability to think. Excitement skittered along her skin, danced through her chest, and nestled in her core, radiating a delicious ache.

The snow fell in earnest by the time they drove up her driveway. Not that it mattered. She could barely breathe with what awaited her.

She flexed her hand one last time on his thigh, scraping her nails to his knee as she reached for the garage door remote. His grip tightened on the steering wheel when he hissed her name.

She batted her eyelashes. "What?"

Pulling on the handbrake, he slipped his fingers around her neck and tugged her closer. He didn't break eye contact while he lowered his head, brushed his lips across hers, plucked her bottom lip until she parted her mouth, then swooped in. The taste of him flexed her fingers, crackling the remote in her hand.

The swipe of his tongue across hers, the softness of his lips, and his ragged breathing scattered her heartbeat. She succumbed, unable to resist him, his magical kisses, the sheer joy of being desired...by him.

He broke away, his gaze fixed on her upturned face. "Blue," he rasped, cupping her cheek to run his thumb along her jaw. He winced and dropped his hand. "You have a visitor."

Chapter Thirteen

Navy squeaked. "A what?"

Gently, Oli steered her jaw to face forward. There, hogging all the space, sat a silver SUV.

"I...wasn't expecting anyone." She scrambled out once Oli placed the car in park. Circling the strange vehicle, she searched for clues as to who this person could be. "A burglar wouldn't park, would he?"

Oli tapped the rental agency's sticker on a window. "I'd like to know how they got in?"

"I keep a spare key under Mom's garden gnome on the porch." She gasped. "Only you or...Gray would know." She bolted, shoving her way into her home.

Every clue sparked joy and an overwhelming hope. The luggage on the floor, obstructing the entryway, the coat thrown over the back of the couch instead of hung on a hook, the empty tub of ice cream on the kitchen counter? Spinning, she threw herself into Oli's arms, tears flowing.

"He's here."

Oli rubbed her back. "Make sure first."

She left his embrace to meet his gaze, taking a moment to wipe her cheeks. "You're right."

Striding down the hallway, she called her brother's name. No response. When she reached Oli's bedroom, sprawled diagonally across his bed was Gray. His sun-bleached curls tumbled over a weathered brow. A scruffy beard hid half his face, and he snored like an overheated rhinoceros.

She jumped up and down, squealing in silence. When Gray huffed, she crept to Oli hovering in the doorway. Shutting the door behind her, she whispered, "How did he know where to find me?"

"I texted him, of course." Oli gathered her against him, sliding his hands down her back to grab her ass.

She wiggled in his embrace. Energy stormed along her veins. She couldn't stand still to save her life.

He spun her, pressing her against the wall. Layering his body over hers, he held her in place. "With as much as I want you, I hate to say this. Gray's in the house, Blue."

She paused, gripping and releasing Oli's biceps. Chewing on her bottom lip, she weighed the chances of Gray finding her in a compromising...um, position. She blinked at Oli, who waited for her decision. Her chest swelled. Swirling her hips, she brushed across his incredible hard-on.

"I can be quiet."

His slow smile fluttered her heartbeat. "Let me park the car." He kissed her temple, lingering for a second before pulling away.

Navy blinked after him, allowing her gaze free rein. His jacket hid his ass, but that didn't matter, not when what awaited her was better than any sex scene she'd ever written. Dashing for her room, she kicked off her shoes, then hesitated. Maybe he wanted to undress her?

Holy sugar, no. She needed him now. Waiting another five minutes for him to peel her pants off would be torture. Besides, if she hurried, she could check her orders. If she was lucky, she could sleep in past dawn. Naked beneath her nightshirt, she fluffed her hair and sprinted for her study, sinking into the chair while her laptop powered up.

Opening her ideas book, she hurried to capture what swirled in her core, how breathless and aflutter she was, what her hopes for the evening entailed. Hands cupping her shoulders snapped her out of the writing zone, and she twisted to smile at Oli. He'd removed his jacket and unbuttoned his shirt, exposing his ribbed stomach and muscled pecs.

"Ready?" he rasped.

"Yes."

Instead of allowing her to rise, he scooped her into his arms and claimed her office chair. Sitting on his lap, staring forward, she wiggled, trying to face him. He tightened an arm around her waist while using his knees to spread her legs wide.

"Oli?" She gripped his arm, heat burning her cheeks when air cooled her inner thighs.

He released her to slide his hand up her nightshirt. She shivered at the brush of his fingers. He cupped her sex but did nothing else. His warm hand added to the throb building inside her.

He slipped a finger into her, drawing a whimper when the need intensified. "Were you wearing panties tonight?"

She shook her head, biting her lip. He swirled her nub. She dug her nails into her thighs. An aching spiraled outward, twitching her knees.

He cupped a breast, plucking a taut nipple through her nightshirt. She ground her hips as his speed increased, driving her toward an orgasm. She panted, squeezing and releasing her knees, then twisted, trying to capture his mouth for a kiss.

He jerked back, chuckling. "Greedy little minx."

She didn't have long to pout with need pounding her senses. "So close," she whispered.

"I know," he smiled then nipped her ear.

The stimulation was too much. The sharp bite of pain on her earlobe soothed by a lick tossed her over the edge. She bit her lip, muffling a scream. Pleasure engulfed her, a wave of intense heat and satisfaction arching and slumping her against him.

"I could fuck you right now," he growled.

Holy sugar, she was so out of depth here. To hell with it, she was claiming him. Mercilessly, she rubbed her backside across his hard-on. "Please do."

He grabbed her hips, holding her still. "No condoms."

She leaned forward and opened the top drawer. "Research." Sorting through the boxes, she chose one and waved it at him.

"Mm, I will be investigating that drawer soon." Before she could settle onto his lap, he rose, clutching her against his chest. A few of his steps carried her into her room. He lowered her until her feet touched the floor. Without a word, he closed and locked her bedroom door.

When he whipped off his shirt, she bounced away to sit cross-legged on the bed, content to watch him strip. He toed off his shoes, peeled off his socks, then unbuckled and unzipped his jeans.

She chuckled. "No underwear, Mr. Trent?"

He smirked. "Around you? Impossible."

Her cheeks warmed under his blatant admiration. Then all thoughts scattered when he dropped his jeans. She parted her mouth on an 'oh,' her gaze fixed on his twitching cock.

"You're overdressed, Blue." He prowled toward her, rippling muscle and sexual promise at its finest.

"Sorry." She tugged off her shirt, tossing it onto the floor.

He paused, his knee on the bed, his gaze fixed on her. The urge to cover herself gripped her, but she only had two arms. Maybe the past year's extra bowls of ice cream and second servings of toasted ciabattas weren't wise. Where he had a hardcore physique, she was more...doughy? She swallowed a giggle. *Baking pun intended.*

"Gorgeous." He trailed a finger over her stomach's bumps and dips to a breast, cupping it to run his thumb back and forth across the nipple. Electricity shot outward. She threw her head back, closed her eyes, and savored the sweet joy of anticipation.

His touch ceased, and paper crinkled. Watching him work a condom on had to be the most sensual thing she'd ever seen. That would definitely be going into one of her novels.

"So are you...gorgeous, I mean." She winced. Shyness struck. The urge to facepalm twitched her fingers. This was Oli. He liked her silliness.

He laughed and lunged, sprawling her back. Every inch of him coated her and sank her deeper into the mattress. He didn't break eye contact when he lowered his lips to hers. His eyes darkened, emotion swirling and changing. She couldn't read them all, but she did recognize affection.

"I've waited too long for you," he said and nudged her thighs apart with his hips.

She obliged, raising her legs to hook around his ass. This action settled his rigid cock where she needed him to be.

"Days?" she frowned.

"An eternity." He followed those beautiful words by gliding into her, slower than she wanted. His eyelashes fluttered. "Worth it."

Sensations flowed from her core. Filling her, owning her, and changing who she was, as Navy, as his friend. She blinked back tears and succumbed to the slow slide and retreat of his thrusts. *Holy sugar, I've never felt this good.* Every nerve was on alert. Tiny hairs all over his body rose as he carried her to another pinnacle.

Still, he didn't break eye contact, taking the time to stroke her cheek, brush curls off her temple, or steal a sweet kiss.

A tear slipped free. She smiled, letting everything he summoned from within her shine through.

"Am I hurting you, Blue?" Concern twisted his features.

She shook her head. "Incredible. Beautiful."

He chuckled. "Short on words, Ms. Author." Rising, he withdrew, raised her legs so the back of each knee rested on his shoulders, and thrust into her balls deep.

She garbled her scream when stars exploded across her vision. Her stomach clenched, and she writhed under his forceful assault. This was desire—strong, overwhelming, demanding, and consuming. She chanted his name when each thrust triggered mini spasms of delight.

"Oh, fuck," he groaned. "I'm coming." He tightened his grip on her hips and froze, his face contorted with painful pleasure. A low growl escaped, but he met her gaze, his eyes a dark gray.

He pulled out with a shudder and lay beside her, gathering her against him. Cupping her jaw, he steered her mouth to his. A long-drawn-out kiss followed with sweet pecks and tongue forages that stole her breath and rekindled the fire he'd just doused.

Oh, sugar, I'm so in love with him. Tears prickled behind her eyes, and she hastily blinked them away. No, she'd enjoy every moment with him. She'd let the future take care of itself when not a nanosecond of worrying could change the outcome.

"Give me a moment." He disappeared into the bathroom, the tap ran, and when he strode back, she took the time to absorb every inch of him into her memory.

When he sprawled beside her, he rolled her over, hugged her against his body, and wrapped an arm around her. "Sweet dreams, my Blue."

"Night," she whispered, drowning in the roiling emotions within her.

Women weren't like men. She couldn't sleep after the most epic sex she'd ever had. Snuggling into his embrace, she tried to distract herself with cupcake ideas. With a sigh, she tucked her hand under the pillow and prayed for sleep.

~*~

Not a chance in hell was Oliver sleeping, not with Blue in his arms and the languid satisfaction of an all-powerful orgasm still catapulting along his senses. She had no clue how he felt about her. He'd loved her for years, but what pinged around his chest was more than that. Each second he spent with her deepened his love for her.

After tonight, her beneath him, and that she'd given of herself without hesitation? Thrusting into her was the culmination of his decade-long fantasy. Still, it wasn't enough. As he'd suspected, fucking her wasn't what he'd been after, although, no woman he'd slept with could compare. No, he needed her heart.

He'd have to reveal his motives and intentions. Antony had ogled her like a starved man. If Oliver was in that man's shoes, he wouldn't give up that easily. Sure, Blue had no intention of dating the man. Oliver needed Antony to realize this. Tammy too, who seemed to think she could preen and stroke Antony's arm to make Oliver jealous.

He smirked and cuddled Blue closer. Those two needed to get with each other and leave him and Blue alone. He hummed. Now that was a good idea.

Which left Gray. How to tell his best friend and possible brother that he was in love with his probably half-sister? How to tell Gray who his real father might be? Oliver winced. That was tomorrow's problem. Blue had suggested they do it together.

"I love you, Blue," he whispered when her breathing deepened. "More now than a second, hour, day, week, month, and year ago."

Her mumbled, "I love you too," stole the air out of his lungs.

His joy was swift to rise and fall. He wanted to wake her and demand if she meant it as a friend or more? She slept on, unaware of his inner turmoil. Tomorrow, it would have to be, but how to word it. With the long hours of night looming, he tucked the blankets around them and gathered her close. Perhaps, instead of rehearsing, what if he spoke from the heart?

He snorted. *Now* that *is a silly idea.*

Chapter Fourteen

OLIVER AWOKE TO AN empty bed. Testing for lingering warmth, he found none. Muted bangs and thumps originated from the kitchen. He smiled. Blue baked. If the sounds hadn't alerted him, the rich aroma of baking bread did. He stretched, then rubbed his morning hard-on. Best to ready himself for the day before Gray woke up.

He considered letting his friend find him naked in Blue's bed. But with the doubtful parentage hanging over them, he didn't want to rock the boat. He clambered out of bed and tugged his pants on. A quick straightening of the duvet and blankets made the bed. He stared at it, a silly grin splitting his cheeks. Before they revealed anything to Gray, Oliver needed a kiss. He hovered at the end of the passage, leaning his shoulder on the wall to admire Blue as she worked.

His chest swelled with the familiar warmth, intensity, and glow that was his love for her.

He smothered a snort. How naïve had he been when he'd thought fleeing her would stop his growing affection? Their lives were forever entwined even if he moved on.

Her head whipped up, and she smiled.

His breath caught. Cue climatic music with a full orchestra, machines pumping out billows of smoke, the spotlight shining on her face, and the camera zooming in on her plump lips.

"Morning." Pink bloomed on her cheeks, but she dipped her head, wiped her hands on a cloth, and jogged to him.

He caught her and crushed her to his chest. "Blue," he rasped, the emotions squeezing his heart in a vise strangled his voice.

She stroked his jaw and kissed him. Heat exploded in his innards, and he spun to pin her to the wall with his hips. He splayed one hand beside her head and cupped her neck with the other, caressing her throat with his thumb. Her heartbeat fluttered under his fingers.

He pulled back to smile. "Did you sleep well?"

She bit her lip and nodded, but her gaze lowered to his mouth. "We'll have to tell Gray."

"Jumping right in?" Oliver swirled his hips to rub the hardest part of him with the hottest part of her.

She gasped. Leaning her head back, she closed her eyes and rotated her hips in return. "The townsfolk think we're dating."

"We *are* dating." He pressed his temple to hers. "I thought you meant the Pops-and-Lorraine thing."

"That too."

"So, over breakfast, we blurt out everything?" He winced. *Poor Gray.*

She stilled. Her eyes darkened, and pain flitted across her face. "I wasn't sure if sex—"

"We're dating, as in girlfriend-boyfriend. Last night wasn't a one-night stand, Blue."

She grimaced despite her eyes warming to their usual blue. Slumping against the wall, she offered him a smile. "I...didn't want to assume. Girlfriend?"

He beamed. "Yup, so we better tell Gray."

"I'll start on breakfast. Bacon and waffles okay?" She rubbed his upper arms to his shoulders and down again.

He shivered, desire pebbling his nipples. "Okay? It's perfect." He gave her nose a quick kiss. "Like you." Releasing her, he gripped her hips to ensure she didn't lose her balance.

"Charmer." Her chuckle jiggled her breasts, drawing his attention.

The temptation to throw her over his shoulder forced him to take another step back.

"Quit looking at me like that, Oli. Go wake Gray."

"Yes, ma'am." He saluted with two fingers to his temple.

She laughed. "And put on a shirt. I can only resist so much."

"Oh?" He arched a brow, captured her hand, and held it against his chest. "You like this?"

She twirled her thumb. "Yes, I like this…" Dragging her hand free, she trailed her fingers down, dipping into his belly button and out to the waistband of his pants.

He expected her to stop there, but she didn't. His breath escaped in a grunt when she cupped his hard-on, giving it a squeeze and a stroke through the denim. Delicious heat shot out from her touch to nestle deep in his core. His balls twinged with eagerness.

"You're playing with fire, Ms. Sanders."

Her brow arched. "Sue me, Mr. Trent." She snatched her hand back when a shower switched on. "You're up."

"I am." He smirked.

"Oli." She pursed her lips.

"Blue." He grinned, unrepentant. "If Gray wasn't here, where would you be?"

Her eyes widened. "Under you," she whispered.

"Damn straight." Taking pity on her, he pressed a kiss to her temple and shifted away…like three steps back. "Okay if I use your shower?"

She nodded while sliding along the hallway toward the kitchen. "I'll use it after break-fast. I didn't want to wake you."

Oliver turned on a heel and strode to his 'old' room to collect his things. He flicked a glance at the bathroom door and chuckled. Gray's unexpected arrival was the best intrusion ever. Sure, Blue couldn't scream as she unraveled in Oliver's arms, but he had a lifetime ahead to draw orgasms from her. What mattered most was that she'd become his last night. Second base? Fuck that. He'd hit a home run, out of the park, and into the stratosphere. The only thing that would send his soul into the cosmos was if she agreed to marry him.

No. He paused while folding a shirt into his luggage before zipping it closed. *If she loves you,* he whispered.

He sighed and hurried to her room. While he dressed after a quick shower, he tilted his head to listen to the muffled voices. With his boots thumping on the hardwood floor, he strode down the hallway, dreading the next hour.

"Morning." He offered his hand to Gray seated on a barstool. "About time you ar-rived."

"I'm a little jetlagged." Gray grinned, his gray eyes twinkling despite the shadows under them. "It's good to be home though." He gestured to the house. "Love this, sis."

"Same," she said, sliding a coffee in front of him. "Coffee, Oli?"

"Please." He chose a stool beside Gray, even as he admired the pull of her shirt across her breasts. "Pops should be up in a few days."

Gray arched a brow, his lips pursed on a sip of coffee. "Good." His tone hardened.

Oliver frowned. "Bad trip?"

"Not at all." Gray's focus shifted to Blue. "Sis, while the waffle maker does its thing, there are gifts beside my bed."

"What?" Her eyes widened, and pure joy brightened her face. She shook her head, though. "It can wait."

Gray's chuckle sounded forced. "Can it?"

Oliver switched a worried glance between him and Blue. Why did Gray want her gone?

She squealed and darted down the hallway.

Oliver's gaze trailed her until she disappeared into the guest room. Fiery agony exploded across his jaw. He stumbled off the stool. Gripping his jaw, he faced Gray. "What the fuck?"

"What the fuck? She's my sister, Oli." Gray raised his fists, readying to swing again.

Oliver grimaced. This was not how he wanted to tell his best friend, but in hindsight, Gray would've reacted this way no matter how Oliver broke the news. "I fucking love her, Gray. I have since she turned sixteen."

Gray paled and dropped his arms. "Seriously?" He rubbed a hand over his face. "She's my sister."

"Like I don't know that." Oliver sliced a glance down the hallway, expecting Blue to join them at any moment. He squeezed Gray's shoulder. "I tried to forget her, to move on... As you can see, it didn't work."

Gray's breath rushed out of him. "If she's going to marry someone, I'd rather it be you. And it had better be marriage you're thinking." He glanced at Blue as she scampered toward them. "Does she know?"

Oliver shook his head. "I *was* helping her make some guy jealous."

Gray's lips twitched, then laughter erupted. "Dude, how bad do you have it?"

Oliver shushed him. "So far, my strategy's working."

"Right." Gray snorted. "Looks like I'll be playing matchmaker this trip."

Oliver jerked back. "Fuck no. Butt out. I've got this."

"Sure you do." Gray smirked.

"Did you flip the bacon?" Blue asked while throwing her arms around Gray. Ethnic bangles in brass and wood jingled whenever she moved. "Love these, but you knew I would." She rolled a bead with a forefinger before catching a tear just under her eye.

Oliver tended to the bacon, keeping his hands busy. He wanted to hug her something fierce. She'd reacted the same with the scarf he'd given her for her sixteenth birthday. He'd received a kiss on the cheek in thanks.

"Oli, sit." She tried to nudge him aside.

He stood firm. "I can do bacon, Blue. You do the waffles. Tell Gray about Sugar Momma's."

She gasped. Excitement twinkled her eyes as she filled Gray in on what she'd planned for her life. Oliver watched, basking in her *joie de vivre*, and dreamed of being there with her when she reopened the bakery.

"Got a man in your life?" Gray winked at Oliver.

Fuck, no. He gritted his teeth, sliced a glance at Blue, then paper-toweled the excess oil off the bacon.

"Not until recently." Her gaze met Oliver's.

"So you've been on dates?" Gray overdid the dramatic frown. "How serious is it? When do I get to meet him?"

"It's serious," Oliver said, then rolled his lips when Gray glared him into silence.

"Dates, Blue? Spill." Gray folded his arms across his chest.

She huffed. "I don't need an older brother anymore, Gray."

"So no to the dates? Listen here, sis, if the ass can't find his balls in his lady purse to ask you out, then he isn't good enough for you." He winked at Oliver, who dropped his head into his palm.

"My thoughts exactly. Turns out he's an ass and shit in bed."

Oliver stilled, ice exploding in his chest. Did she mean him or Antony? "What?"

"Like I can't see through you two?" She tapped a foot. "Neither of you are good at acting. When did you tell him, Oli? How long have you known, Gray?"

"Known what?" Gray opted for innocence.

Bad play. Oliver rubbed his jaw and winced.

"That Oli and I are...dating." She paused to run a gaze over him, pressing the tip of her tongue to her top lip as she blushed. "We were supposed to tell him together."

Gray chuckled. "I've known for ten minutes, and he didn't need to say a word. The damn man looks at you like you're his personal Shangri-La."

"Oh." She blinked at Oliver then hurriedly placed a heaped plate in front of Gray. "Fake dating was supposed to make another guy jealous, but that man turned out to be an ass."

"Fake?" Gray growled around a mouthful of syrup-drenched waffle.

She nodded while scooping waffles onto another plate. "Yeah, until last night."

"Why?" He whipped his head up, bacon balancing on a fork. "What happened last night?"

Oliver froze, then reached for his coffee when a bite of waffle lodged in his throat. Telling Gray they were doing *it* would be too much.

"Asshat propositioned me." Blue tore off a chunk of bacon with her teeth, chewing while she made fresh coffee.

"I for one am happy he's out of the picture," Oliver wheezed.

"We're still on for dancing, right?" She nibbled her lip. "I mean, the point was to make him jealous. We could stay in and watch movies...or something."

Hell, no, he'd dreamed of spinning her around a dance floor, their bodies brushing, their arms entwined. "I'd be honored to spend the evening with you, Blue."

Tears shimmered on her eyelashes, but she sniffed and wiped them away. His heart wrenched, and the urge to hug her gripped him again.

She bit into a slice of waffle dripping syrup, taking a moment to lick her lips. "Gray, are you coming with us?"

Oliver glowered at Gray, promising hell if he joined them.

He threw up his hands. "As much as I'd love to, sis, I'm exhausted."

"I get it. Oli and I will go, but we won't stay out too late. I'm hopping into the shower. Help yourself to coffee." She jogged down the hallway. "We need to talk about Mom," she called before closing her bedroom door.

Oliver stared after her, wishing he could ask about her crying.

Gray sucked on his thumb, then flicked his hair off his temple with his pinkie. "Maybe come clean?"

"And what? Lose her for good?" Oliver pushed his plate aside.

"You have it bad." Gray helped himself to Oliver's half-finished waffle. "How did you hide it from me for so long?"

"It was easy in the beginning. She wouldn't talk to me after I stopped her and Ronnie Landon from kissing."

His best friend stared at him. Oliver squirmed, not used to being under Gray's scrutiny. "Jealousy?"

"Yup." Oliver sighed. "A ferocious green monster I couldn't control." He tried for a shrug but gave up. "And setting up our business took most of my time."

"Keeping my ass alive, you mean."

Oliver smiled. "Yeah, something like that."

Gray threw his arm across Oliver's shoulders. "Welcome to the family."

Oliver frowned. "Got to win her heart first." Family? He finished his last piece of bacon. Yeah, there was still that to discuss.

Chapter Fifteen

Navy, with tears slipping free, closed the door and leaned against it. She bit her fist, hoping to calm her ragged breathing. It would be his honor? Who spoke like that? Swiping her cheeks, she sighed and pushed off the door. The man she loved, that's who.

She should be ecstatic about dating Oli, but things had happened so fast. Yeah, she should have waited, not had sex on their first date. Not that she regretted last night. She rubbed a sweaty palm on her thigh.

She huffed and stripped. "Don't overthink things, Navy."

So dancing was still on. She activated the water and ducked under it as soon as it heated. Would dressing to impress win his heart? She shrugged while lathering the bar of soap. Not that she had a choice. She had to give this her all. Besides, she wanted to look pretty for him.

As she washed, shampooed, and rinsed, she mentally sifted through her wardrobe. Despite having a dress in mind, she wanted to be certain. Stepping out of the shower, she dried her body and rubbed her hair, planning her shoes, accessories, and make-up. Snorting, she tossed the towel aside and strolled naked from the bathroom. And squealed.

"Now that's a beautiful sight." Oli chuckled.

"Oli," she whispered, snatching clothes out of her closet, uncaring what they were. The way he ran his gaze over her had her insides knotting. Her nipples recalled his touch. Her sex longed for his thrusts. "What are you doi—?"

"Gray had to make a few calls." Oli caught her hands as soon as she clipped on a bra. "I wanted to check on you." He dipped his head, maintaining eye contact despite her being naked from the waist down.

She shuffled closer, using him to hide her nudity. One would think after last night, shyness wouldn't surface. "I'm fine. Why would you think—?"

"You were on the verge of crying, Blue." He circled his arms around her and crushed her against him. With his chin on the crown of her head, he continued, "You know you can talk to me about anything, right?"

She snorted, drawing in a wealth of his sinfully delicious cologne. "How about letting me dress?"

He chuckled. "No. I'm undecided on whether there's time for a licking."

She gasped and suppressed a shudder.

He spun her on the spot and swatted her backside.

She smothered a squeal but reached for her jeans, wiggling them on before he made true on his threat. If Gray wasn't home... She snuck glances at Oli, who'd settled on the edge of her bed, his focus fixed on her.

"So spill. Why the tears? Happy Gray's home?"

What could she say? That she was head over heels in love? *Sugar, no.* "Yes." She whipped her baggy blouse over her head.

As soon as her chin cleared the collar, she stilled.

Oli had risen to his feet and crowded her. "I don't like it when you hide things from me, Blue."

She huffed. "Like you hide things from me?" Arching a brow, she splayed her fingers on his chest, wanting to shove him back. But he covered her hand with his, looped his arm around her waist, and in a smooth move, sat with her on his lap.

Twisting her head to look at him shot pain up her neck, so she pulled away to stand. She wasn't a little girl eager for Santa's attention, nor was she a slim woman. When she rose, he tugged her down. She shifted to sit sideways, meeting his gaze. Resting her hand against his chest, she relished the thick muscle beneath her touch and the heat pouring off him.

His eyes had darkened, and the intensity within them snatched her breath. Tears pressed at the backs of her eyes, and she bit her lip, frantically searching for a subject change.

"How sure are you that this hunting lodge will work? I mean, it's a noble idea, Oli, but intentions have a way of deteriorating."

He studied her, his gaze traversing her face to settle on her lips. "They do, but you'll be here to keep me on the straight and narrow." He caressed her cheek from jaw to earlobe where he buried his fingers in her hair. "How about I make you a partner? That way you have a say over policies and the running of the lodge."

She squirmed, tearing a groan from him. He released her but gripped her hips. When she tried to rise, he held her in place.

"Sit still, Blue, you're making me rethink not licking you."

She froze and shot a glance at the closed bedroom door. Before he could stop her, she spun and straddled his lap, resting her knees at his hips. "Just like that, make me a partner? Don't I have to invest or something?"

He grabbed her ass and squeezed. When he spoke, his voice was hoarse. "How much cash do you have on you?"

She shrugged. "Twenty-two dollars, I think."

He captured her chin between forefinger and thumb. "Sold." His gaze settled on her mouth again.

She huffed, trying to ignore her tingling lips. "I do have savings. Even with the cost of the Sugar Momma's revamp."

She fought the urge to arch and purr when he trailed his hands up and down her back.

His lips twisted into a smirk. "We can dip into that when the lodge has quiet months."

She paused and studied his hazel eyes. The burst of brown and gray against the green still fascinated her. "Are we doing this?"

"Yup. I'm serious, Blue." And he was. She knew that look, the same one he'd worn when his mother died.

"Fine, release me. Let's find Gray."

Oli's grin warmed his eyes and dimpled his cheeks. Her heart fluttered, and she lowered her chin to hide the heat crawling to her hairline. When he flung out his arms, she climbed off his lap, using his shoulders as leverage.

He followed. "We should tell him about your writing."

"Why?" she squeaked, then shook her head. "Let's not overwhelm him."

"I say tell him. His parentage matters far more than your incredible stories." He sat at the kitchen island, resting his elbows on the counter.

She glanced at Gray pacing the porch and without a jacket on like the cold didn't bother him. "Fine." She huffed. "Coffee?" A fresh pot for when Gray came inside would be appreciated.

When Oli didn't answer, she shifted her focus. He stared at her, something swirling in his eyes that spun her vision. Her heart fluttered. Was that love or affection? A spark of heat shot down her spine and twitched her fingers. She opened her mouth to ask but hesitated. What if he didn't love her like she wanted? Any future dates or family gatherings would be awkward.

Keeping busy would help. She brewed the coffee and tackled the remaining dishes. Oli didn't speak, but his gaze trailed her around the kitchen.

"Is that coffee I smell?" Gray grinned as he closed the door behind him, rubbing his hands together like it was chilly and not below zero outside.

"Don't be an idiot. Wear a jacket." She tutted as she slid refilled mugs of coffee onto the island. "Now, ready to talk about Mom?"

Gray's smile faded, but he nodded and chose a stool. "Is she ill?"

"No," she said. "She's in perfect health."

"We saw her yesterday. She took one look at me and called me Eddie." Oli stirred his coffee and took a sip. "Seems she and Eddie had a thing twenty-nine years ago."

"What?" Gray gripped his mug. "No, Mom wouldn't have cheated on Dad."

"That's what we thought too." Navy gestured with a flick of her fingers between her and Oli. "It's just that she claimed you're Eddie's."

Gray stilled, his face paling. "Eddie's what?" His voice was hoarse.

"As in my half-brother," Oli all but whispered.

"But Mom's memory is—"

"I know." Navy squeezed Gray's wrist. "Which is why we thought we'd get a DNA test to make sure."

"What? Why?" Gray folded his arms across his chest.

"If Eddie's your biological father, wouldn't you want to spend time with him?" She would, without a doubt. Eddie had been there for her after Dad had died. She already thought of him as her surrogate father.

"Does he know?" Gray glanced at Oli.

"No." Oli frowned. "If it's not true, then I don't want to break his heart."

Gray thumped his chest. "But it's okay to drag me through this trauma?"

Navy threw her arms up. "For sugar's sake, Gray, it's not as if we're asking for a kidney. Don't you want to know?"

"Dad was my father, Eddie is yours, Oli. I mean, I do see Eddie as a father figure, just not my real dad, y'know." Gray ran a trembling hand over his face. "Couldn't Mom have remembered wrong?"

Navy shrugged. "It's possible, which is why we wanted to test your DNA." She circled the island to slide into Oli's arms. He cradled her against him. "We could forget it, Oli. I mean, knowing won't change the dynamics of our family."

Oli pursed his lips. "I'd want to know, but yeah, I guess we could."

Right, time for another subject change. She sucked in a deep breath. "And, on a less serious note, I'm a published author."

Gray nodded, smacking his lips around a sip of coffee. "I know."

She gasped. "What? How?" She faced Oli. "You told him?" With a shake of her head, she warred with logic. Oli had said he wouldn't and was a man she trusted to keep his word. "I'm sorry. I didn't mean to doubt—"

"You told Oli before me?" Gray sliced a furious glare between them. "I left Colefield, Navy, but I still keep tabs on you."

"No one but Tina—" She dropped her head in her hands. "Oh." When Tina came back, there'd be a reckoning. Spinning, Navy threw her arms around Oli, who had yet to react to her accusation.

"It's okay, Blue." He pressed a kiss to her temple. "You can make it up to me later," he whispered in her ear, his warm breath sending goosebumps along her skin.

"Anything else?" At Gray's arched brow, Navy tucked her bottom lip under the top one. "Good. We'll never mention this DNA nonsense again. And, sis, I expect autographed copies of your novels on my bed by tonight." He rose, downed his coffee, and glanced at Oli. "Let's inspect our investment."

Oli nodded. "I'll meet you by the SUV."

As soon as Gray strolled into the garage while pulling his jacket on, Oli captured her chin and raised her lips to his. He didn't kiss her like she longed for: hot, needy, assuaging yet stoking the fires within. Instead, his kiss was sweet, lingering, his touch reverent.

He set her aside with a squeeze of her hips. "I'll have my lawyer draw up the partnership papers. Don't spend the twenty-two dollars you owe me." He tugged his jacket on, a smile teasing his luscious mouth. "We'll pick up pizza for dinner. And," with a trail of his gaze down her body, "dancing's at eight."

As soon as the garage door closed, she slumped against the counter. Her knees trembled, her lips tingled, and her emotions swung like a pendulum. This morning hadn't gone as she'd expected. She was half-tempted to steal Gray's DNA and have it tested on the sly. Then again, knowing and not being able to share? No, it was wiser to do as he asked.

"Well, fuck me." She gasped and slapped a hand across her mouth. "No need to go all potty-mouthed on me, Navy. Get your shit together." She sighed then stacked the pies, tarts, and loaves of bread, ready for delivery.

Chapter Sixteen

DINNER WITH HER BROTHER and Oli over pizza while watching a Nat Geo documentary on rhinos reminded Navy of her youth. How carefree they'd been, with no worries in life, as Mom brought them snacks while scolding Gray for putting his legs on her imported Imbuia coffee table.

The sad plight of the rhinos couldn't still the excitement in Navy. What helped distract her from her impending date with Oli was Gray's inside information on how policies had changed and to what lengths the countries went in the hopes of saving the few remaining rhinos. The credits rolled, and she dutifully gasped and awed at her brother's name scrolling past.

"Well, we should get ready?" Gray rubbed his palms up and down his thighs. "I could do with a night out."

Oli glowered. "I thought you said you were tired."

Gray shrugged. "Someone's got to chaperone my sister and keep an eye on you." He slapped his knee. "Just kidding." He leapt to his feet and strolled down the hallway. "Just practice safe sex."

"I'm going to kill him," Oli said through gritted teeth.

Navy chuckled. "Why? We do use condoms."

His gaze warmed as he smiled. "Yes, we do."

"On that note, let me...um, dress for tonight." She bolted, abandoning Oli before she climbed him like a stripper pole.

Dancing wasn't necessary when they could spend the night under the sheets, but it had been ages since she'd been to the club. When she closed the bedroom door, she squealed, stomped her feet, and shook her head.

His luggage snagged her attention. What they needed to discuss was sleeping arrangements. She assumed he'd bunk with her, which meant he was supposed to dress in her room. She swung the door open to find him standing there, his hand raised.

A lopsided grin twisted his lips. "I need my things."

She stepped back. "Want to get ready in here?"

He jerked back. "You don't mind?"

She grabbed his hand and pulled him inside. "I'll shower first."

"We could share a shower..." His gaze heated as he studied her. "Never mind. For tonight, I'll use Gray's room." Before she could speak, he'd hauled his luggage out of her room. He hesitated at the door. "Don't think because I'm walking away that I don't want to taste every fucking inch of you, Blue. I do, all the damn time." He snapped the door shut.

She grinned while fanning her flushed face. *All the damn time?* Oh, she loved that. She dressed on a buzzing high with moments lost to a silly smile or a deep sigh. While putting on her earrings, she studied her reflection. Holy sugar, she looked good. The royal blue dress crisscrossed her body in wide swaths of fabric. The off-the-shoulder bodice dipped, exposing a decent amount of cleavage. The dress, stopping just below her knee, pinned every bump and jiggle in place and cupped her breasts with a built-in bra. She paused to catch her breath, fluffed her curls one last time, then grabbed a bronze-colored clutch.

With her shoes in hand, she hurried down the hallway and smiled when she found Oli waiting.

"Is this too much?" She placed the clutch on the counter to run a damp palm along a hip, her gaze fixed on his face.

He raised his head and blinked. His nostrils flared while his eyes darkened with something hot and intense. He pushed himself off the couch and strode toward her, his jeans pulling tight across his sculpted thighs.

"Fuck, Blue. This is... You look... Shit." He splayed his hand over his heart, his button-up white shirt striking against his skin.

"Right." She laughed. "Shit is bad?"

His eyes widened. "No. Stunning... Gorgeous." His voice deepened. "Incredibly sexy."

"Better." She crossed to him and touched his forearm to slip her transparent peep-toe slingback platforms on.

He groaned. "Those shoes—"

"Are shit too?" She chuckled.

He smirked. "Tease me to your heart's content, Blue, but you in that dress... I'm still peeling my tongue off the floor."

She adjusted her breasts. Without the sensation of straps, she couldn't shake the sensation that her babies sagged. "I can change into something less—"

"Don't you fucking dare." He cupped her cheek, then trailed a finger along her collarbone. She shivered at his touch, relishing the texture of his skin against hers and the zing of fire he left behind. "I'll have to beat them off with sticks."

"Them?" She arched a brow. "Colefield is a little sparse men-wise. You'll have to dance with me, Oli." She broke into Mr. Roboto. "Like this?"

He scoffed. "I can dance, Blue."

Gripping her hips, he tugged her into his arms and shuffled to no music, sliding his pelvis across hers. Her breath caught, and to hide her nipples pebbling, she closed the distance between them, clung to his shoulders, and let him lead. His cologne filled her nose—heated by his skin made it more addictive. Where he touched, where his fingers lingered, sparked fire along her nerve endings.

"I..." She cleared her throat and tried again. "I need to put lipstick on, then we can go."

"Plenty of time," he mumbled and pressed her temple to his chest.

She snuggled deeper, letting him shuffle her around the kitchen, lounge, and dining room. Engulfing her, besides the warmth of his body, was this incredible peace.

He ran his hands down her back to her ass, then jerked away. "Fuck, Blue, I want to kiss you so much right now." He flicked trembling fingers at her purse. "Lipstick."

She opened her mouth to beg for a kiss. Despite the burn on her cheeks in memory of the one he'd given her that morning, she didn't know what to say. *Hell, yes, kiss the sugar out of me?* Soon, she had to tell him she loved him, but not now. Thrusting aside her nervousness, she found her lipstick, and in the hall mirror, applied the crimson color.

He watched her glide it on, wincing when she rolled her lips.

"Shit," he whispered. "That's worse." Layering his chest to her back, he slipped his arms around her waist and rested his chin on her shoulder to meet her gaze in the mirror. "The color suits you, Blue, but fuck, couldn't you choose something less...seductive?"

He kissed her neck and bolted to the door, taking their coats off the hooks along the way. "When Gray's asleep tonight, I promise to adore every inch of you."

She smothered a laugh. The poor man. "I'd love to go dancing, but if you want to stay home...?"

"Don't tempt me," he groaned, holding her coat open for her.

He opted to drive, his knuckles white where they gripped the steering wheel.

"Thank you for tonight." She squeezed his thigh.

He glanced at her before facing forward. "A pleasure." Shifting in his seat, he covered her hand with his. The tension in his body didn't ease.

She frowned. "What's wrong?"

His smile was stiff. "Impatient, that's all. And don't ask me why, Ms. Nosey."

He parked outside *Club Frozen*. The rectangular building was lined on the outside with corrugated metal sheets, inside with wooden paneling. She recalled the bar ran along the back wall. Overlooking the dance floor that extended the length of the club were tables on the upper level. The music boomed, almost deafening when Oli ushered her inside. Her hips twitched as her heart hurried to match the beat. After taking their coats, he led her across the semi-crowded floor to the bar.

Without asking her preference, he ordered a white-wine spritzer—her favorite. While they waited for their drinks, he curled her against his side, his touch gentle yet predatorial. Giddiness summoned a giggle, so she glanced away, hoping for a distraction. Her gaze settled on a glowering Tammy shimmying her ass next to Antony whose heated focus lingered on the blonde woman. So not interested in Navy? Huh.

She gritted her teeth, faked a smile, and waved. "Oh, for sugar's sake, Oli." She snuggled against him, drawing his attention with a tap on his chest. "We have company."

He met her gaze and didn't break eye contact. His arched brow indicated curiosity, but he focused on her as if there was nowhere else he wanted to look. "Antony?"

She nodded and pulled back to accept the glass Oli offered her. "I should have told him no from the start, but I was shocked, pissed, and don't judge me for this, a little flattered." She held her forefinger an inch from her thumb. "Like this much."

"Now you're taken." Oli waited, expectant.

"Yes," she squeaked.

He grinned. "Good." Scooping the can of soda off the bar counter, he escorted her up the stairs to the tables. They chose one close to the railing. She sat on the edge of a chair and peered at the dance floor below.

His attentiveness swirled excitement within her. She'd hoped to look pretty tonight, even though appearances couldn't garner his heart. As she sipped her wine, humming when the cool liquid trickled down her throat, she scanned the crowd below with unseeing eyes. What she should do is confess, right? Just tell him how she felt.

She faced him, opening her mouth to blurt it out before her courage abandoned her.

"May I have this dance?"

She jerked to the side, dragging her gaze from a frowning Oli to Antony. "No." She winced. "Thanks."

A delicate hand stroked Oli's shoulders a second before Tammy sat beside him. "Go on, Navy. It will give me a chance to catch up with Oliver."

Navy blinked at her squeezing Oli's bicep then trailing a path to his neck. A fountain of fire bubbled up, choking her throat, and making her eyes water. She wanted to rip the woman's arm off.

Oli tried to shift away. A pulse ticked at the base of his jaw, and his face hardened into a scowl that rivaled when he'd found Ronnie touching her knee.

This had to stop. She straightened her shoulders and faced Antony. "I'm not interested in anything romantic, Antony. I'm dating Oli and have no intention of dropping him for you. And Tammy, I suggest you get your hands off my man." Navy shot to her feet. "Gray and Oli taught me how to fight, so unless you want to explain to everyone how you got a black eye—"

"Geez, Navy, Antony just wanted one dance." Tammy's false smile didn't fool Navy.

She bit her lip and bulged her eyes at Oli, who did nothing but laugh silently, his shoulders shaking. She huffed. No help was coming from that quarter. She was tempted to walk away and let him handle Tammy on his own. "No offense intended, Tammy. Oli and I are on a date. Intruding is the epitome of rudeness."

Tammy arched a brow. "Epitome? Did you swallow a dictionary?"

Navy balled her fingers into fists, wishing she'd worn flats when she teetered on her heels.

Oli rose, forcing Tammy to let him go. "Dance with me, beautiful." He offered Navy his hand.

She took it, slipped past a fuming Tammy and a nonchalant Antony, and followed Oli onto the dance floor. The music was disco, but it could change at any moment to country or hip-hop—a random selection that played something for everyone.

"Wow." Oli drew her into his arms for a non-disco shuffle. "I fucking love what you just did, Blue."

She snorted, shame and anger still burning her cheeks. "What? Behave like a jealous wife?"

He captured her chin in his hand and kissed her. Moaning, she wrapped her arms around him and opened her mouth, needing his kiss to publicly claim her. Apparently, not the kiss at the butchery or last night's dinner had made any impact on Tammy's plans.

"Next time you want to go dancing, just dress up, and I'll happily shuffle you around our living room."

She nuzzled his chest, loving the brushing of his hips across her torso. "Mm, I'd ask you to take me home...except, Gray's there." With Tammy's gaze boring into Navy, this night had fast lost its luster.

The music switched to hip-hop.

Oli broke away and laced his fingers through hers. "Come, let's get a little air."

He led her to an enclosed patio at the back of the building. A couple sat in the corner, whispering to each other. Oli gathered Navy in his arms and hugged her, resting his chin on the crown of her head. She nestled against him, content to just be. They knew each other so well that words weren't necessary.

The thump-thump of the muted music drew the couple, leaving Navy and Oli alone. She sucked in a shuddering breath and stepped back, preparing to confess how she felt.

"Oli, I need to—"

"Blue, I can't—"

They spoke at the same time and broke off to laugh.

"You go first," she urged.

"All right." He snagged her hand and ushered her to a bench. "I have a confession to make."

She waited, not wanting to interrupt him. Although, she couldn't fathom what he needed to tell her, unless... She froze. He was engaged, married, had kids?

"I knew from the start that Antony wasn't interested in you."

She frowned. "But he is? Or I think he is."

"That came as a surprise. When we visited the fire station, not once did he ogle you." Oli paced while running a hand through his hair. "But I needed a game plan, a way to convince you to date me."

She squeezed her eyes shut for a second, trying to understand what Oli was telling her.

"So this thing with Antony was a game?" she whispered. Had Oli played her? She shook her head, refusing to believe he was that sort of man.

"If by game you mean Russian Roulette with my future and heart at stake, then yes." He gripped her shoulders, his thumbs swirling circles across her skin. "I needed you to see me as more than your research partner and oldest friend."

"Well, I do. Now what?" Her eyes widened when fear wrapped boney fingers around her heart. "We're still friends, right?"

"Always, Blue. We have history, and it molded me into who I am and who we will be." He knelt in front of her but didn't release her shoulders. "I..." He paused, as if he chose his words with care. "Remember when you asked if I'd ever been in love?" He arched his brows and gave her a pointed look.

She frowned, trying to recall that late-night conversation, then gaped, fluttering her hand on her chest. "Me? But you said it was unrequited? That you'd loved her for ages."

"I'm sorry for the pain I caused, Blue. Had I been upfront... I just couldn't bear the thought of Ronnie kissing you. I lost my temper and you at that moment."

"Oli! Since I was *sixteen*?" She didn't blink as she ran her gaze over his face while wringing her hands. "You didn't once say anything. Why now?"

"At Mom's funeral, you were your old self, and it gave me such hope. Then your late-night calls spurred my dream to own the lodge and to move closer to you."

She smiled. "Sex talk drove you to pursue your dreams?"

"No, just hearing your voice made me realize how much I'd missed you, how pointless my absence was, that where I most wanted to be was here with you." He drew in a shuddering breath. "What I'm trying to say is that I'm in love with you, Blue."

Her throat constricted as she struggled to stem the exploding joy inside her. Had she misheard him? Could she ask him to repeat it? She opened her mouth, but what came out was, "I love you too."

"What—?" He stilled, then cupped her cheeks and shuffled closer. "What did you say?"

Through her tears, she managed to squeak, "I love you, Oliver Dylan Trent."

"As more than a friend with benefits?" His nose was an inch from touching hers. His breath warmed her chin, and a smile twitched his lips.

She laughed and slipped her arms over his shoulders. "Yes, I love you as more than my dearest friend."

He crushed his mouth across hers, tears shimmering on his lashes. Liquid heat warmed her insides with blinding joy. His tongue teased hers, and she clung to him, savoring his masterful kisses and the solid feel of him beneath her fingers. The man she loved was all hers for the taking.

"I hoped," he whispered between kisses along her jaw. He gathered her close, and that peace like before flowed over her. "I'm one lucky son of a bitch."

"No more secrets between us." She leaned back to meet his gaze.

"Agreed." He beamed. "Can we leave now?"

She chuckled. "Why? Aren't you having fun?"

"Anywhere with you is fun, Blue, but I ache to kiss every inch of you." He rose, lifting her to her feet as he did so. With his hands on her hips, he kept her against him.

"But Gray's still home."

Oli sighed. "I yearn to hold you, Blue. As long as I can do that, then I'll be a patient man." He laced their fingers and tugged her across the dance floor. "As soon as I ask Gray for permission, I plan to marry you, Navy."

"What?" she gasped, pretty sure she'd misheard him. The beat and chatter of the club garbled his voice.

He said no more while helping her into her coat, but when they stepped into the parking lot, he faced her. "I want to marry you and not waste another minute of my life without you."

She grinned, unable to deny how much she adored him. "Do I have a say?"

"Yup." He ushered her into the passenger seat. "Where, when, and who can attend. Other than that, no." After a tap on her nose, he circled the hood, unplugged the SUV, then climbed into the driver's seat. "Any objections, future Mrs. Navy Anna Trent?"

"Not a one, Oli." She settled her hand on his thigh and smiled. "I'm all yours."

He raised her hand from his thigh to kiss her knuckles. "As I am yours."

Epilogue

Have you ever been in love?

Oliver grinned at his phone, droning out Pops grumbling about the construction delays. They'd moved into the lodge a week ago, but there were items on the snag list he wasn't happy about.

Offering his father his back, Oliver typed his response to Blue. *Yes, with one woman.*

Dots flickered, and he tightened his grip on his phone, impatient for her response. Four blissful months had passed since their club confessions.

Well, this one woman needs you.

He peered at the lodge a few hundred yards away, expecting to see her at the glass double doors. Like the wings of an eagle, the guest rooms sprawled on either side of the common room, reception, kitchen, and dining area. To the far right stood a lone cabin for Pops. Barns, feeding rooms, storerooms, and veterinary rooms sat to the far left. All around them, as far as the eye could see, rolled hills of snow-covered trees stretching to the horizon.

His chest swelled, and he raised his face to the afternoon sunlight.

"Are you listening?" Pops snapped.

"No. Blue needs me."

Pops shook his head but couldn't hide his grin. "The mother of my future grandchildren comes first." He checked his watch. "Besides, I'm off to fetch Lorraine."

Oliver strode to the SUV, leaping into the passenger seat. Dad stomped the snow off his boots before he climbed in, slamming the driver's door.

"Listen, son, there's something I've been meaning to tell you."

Oliver frowned, twisting to meet his father's narrowed gaze.

Pops squeezed and released the steering wheel as if something bothered him. "Um, many years ago, Lorraine and I... well, we kind of... It was just the one night." His face turned red.

"I know."

His father gasped. "You do?"

"Yup, Aunt Lori mistook me for you and confessed."

Pops tucked his bottom lip under his top teeth. "About Gray?"

Oliver squeezed his father's shoulder. "He doesn't want to do a DNA test to confirm it. Says he thinks of you as his father, knowing for sure either way won't change that."

Pops slumped, his breath rushing out, then he started the engine. "Good."

Oliver rubbed his palms along his thighs, eager to reach Blue. She still fired his soul, lighting his heart as she did his life. Now he wanted to share with her that Pops knew. They didn't have to keep it a secret anymore, unconfirmed or not.

"When's Gray back from Greenland? I wanted to ask him about the look-out points and the upcoming open day."

Oliver shrugged. "Drop him a text and maybe tell him you know that he knows."

Pops chuckled. "Will do." He pulled the SUV to a halt outside the reception doors but kept the engine running.

Oliver waved and leapt out, watched his father drive off, then bolted inside. The aroma of apple pie filled the air—cinnamon, sweet, tart—watering his mouth. After removing his jacket, he weaved around the scattered couches, crossed over large native-woven rugs, and passed the reception desk. The crackle of a fire burning in the massive fireplace muffled his footsteps.

At the arched doorway into the kitchen, he paused and leaned against the stone, feasting his gaze on Blue. She hummed as she worked, rolling out dough and folding strips into croissants. The wall of industrial ovens behind her were in various stages of use.

"About time you got here, Oli," she scowled, then ruined her scolding with a laugh.

He circled the island to wrap his arms around her, cupping her belly with his hands. "Turns out your mom told Pops. All's in the open now."

"What?" Blue squeaked.

"Yup." Nuzzling her neck, he pressed kisses then nipped, making her squirm. "Are we going to Tammy and Antony's engagement party?"

Blue shook her head. "I sent an apology and a gift."

Good. His evenings were spent with her and family, just the way he liked it. "Ready for tonight?"

She beamed, her cheeks rosy, her eyes sparkling. "Yes, just got a last-minute order I'm working through, but the tarts, pies, and cakes are done."

He stepped aside to allow her to slide the baking tray into an oven. When she stripped the gloves off, he captured her hand and pulled her close for a kiss. The moment their lips met, that same fire shot through him, like their first kiss on the couch. His heartbeat fluttered, jarring his breathing. He broke the kiss and rested his temple on hers.

"I see you're not engaged anymore, Ms. Navy Sanders." He nudged his head at her sapphire ring resting in an empty butter dish. "I want every man to know you're mine."

Her laughter echoed off the walls and seeped into him. "Not while I'm baking, Oli. Maybe a tattoo instead of a wedding ring? Then it's permanent."

Fuck, I love her. He tightened his arms, careful not to squash her. "It's a pity Gray isn't here for the announcement," Oliver whispered into her hair.

"He's going to love being an uncle." She snuck her fingers under the hem of his shirt, her touch hot. "Got time for a quickie?"

He chuckled. "We have as long as it takes for Pops to fetch your mom." Spinning her to face the back of the kitchen, he swatted her plump and gorgeous ass.

She squealed and shot him a heated glance over her shoulder.

Like a love-sick puppy, he followed her, his mind tossing up images of how he wanted her sprawled before him. Last night, they'd been exhausted, so a quick wham and bam had been it. The way his chest swelled with love for his unborn child and Blue, he planned to take his time and adore every inch of her.

He needed her breathless, pleading, and panting his name.

Closing the kitchen door to their home built at the back of the lodge, he faced his future with eagerness. He'd never imagined he could be this happy.

"Are you coming?" she called, items of her clothing marking a trail.

"Try and stop me," he rasped and shut their bedroom door.

About the Author

Sevannah Storm is a fiction writer who immerses herself in fantastical worlds both magical and science fiction. She has a flare for the creative, having studied art and interior architecture, and spends her time drawing, oil painting, and writing. An avid reader from an early age, Sevannah finds her inspiration from various sources: games, novels, music, and the land of make-believe. The unique versus the practical has brought on numerous debates.

In her spare time, she does Pilates and rereads novels that snatch her breath away. Having embraced the social media world, you can find her on most platforms.

Her home is a land south of Wakanda, where animals roam free. Born in Zimbabwe, she grew up in South Africa. The crisp blue skies with cotton-candy sunsets expand her heart and soul, encapsulating a sense of freedom.

Words she lives by: "Know your pothole and dodge it. Don't work in a pencil factory if you're a vampire."

Sevannah loves to hear from her readers. You can find and connect with her at the links below.

Website/Newsletter:

https://www.sevannahstorm.com/

Facebook:

https://www.facebook.com/sevannah.storm

Instagram:

https://www.instagram.com/sevannah.storm/

Twitter:

https://twitter.com/sevannah_storm

Thank you for taking the time to read *Kissing Navy*. If you enjoyed the story, please tell your friends and leave a review. Reviews support authors and ensure they continue to bring readers books to love and enjoy.